ETHAN

The K9 Files, Book 1

Dale Mayer

Books in This Series:

Ethan, Book 1
Pierce, Book 2

ETHAN: THE K9 FILES, BOOK 1
Dale Mayer
Valley Publishing Ltd.

Copyright © 2019

This is a work of fiction. Names, characters, places, brands, media, and incidents are either the product of the author's imagination or are used fictitiously. Any resemblance to actual events, locales, or persons, living or dead, is entirely coincidental.

ISBN-13: 978-1-773361-30-7
Print Edition

About This Book

When one door closes ... second chances open another ...

Ethan was lost after a major accident abruptly shifted him from a military life to a civilian one, from working with dogs to odd jobs ... In that time, he'd spent months healing from his physical injuries. When he connects with Badger and the rest of his Titanium Corp. group of former SEALs, Badger offers Ethan an opportunity he can't refuse. A chance to do the work he used to do ... with a twist.

Cinnamon works from home as a project manager plus is heavily involved in global dog rescues—dogs of all kinds. When Ethan walks into the next door's vet's office with an injured shepherd in his arms, she sees another lost soul—just like the canine ones she helps.

Ethan knows he's about to take a dangerous step, but he's on the job, and no one—on the job or not—hurts animals while he's around. This poor shepherd has taken enough abuse, and Ethan fears she is only the tip of a nightmare he's determined to uncover. But he knows she's going to lead him in the right direction.

He has his sights set on saving one dog in particular, Sentry: K9 File 01.

Sign up to be notified of all Dale's releases here!

http://dalemayer.com/category/blog/

PROLOGUE

B ADGER WALKED INTO the office for the impromptu meeting and smiled at his friends. "I had a very unusual and cryptic conversation this morning, which is why we are all gathered here."

"You going to tell us about it?" Erick asked, lifting a fresh cup of coffee to his lips.

"No, he is," Badger said, pointing to one wall. "I have Commander Glen Cross on the line." He hit the button on the phone. "Go ahead, Commander. You're on video. What can we do for you?"

The commander's stern countenance filled the screen before them. "Who is that there with you? Identify your-selves."

One by one the men executed a roll call.

The commander, a smile in his voice, said, "Now those are some names to warm my heart. I heard you've started a new company, Titanium Corp, to employ other former SEALs in situations like your own. Is that correct?"

"Yes, that's correct." Badger glanced around the room at the waiting faces. "Is there something we can help you with?"

"Yes, possibly. But only if you have time to volunteer. This is a big-heart mission that unfortunately doesn't come with pay. ... You know how very proud the military is of our K9 program, correct?"

The men nodded.

"Absolutely," Geir said. "We personally have had good reasons to be thankful for that program."

Badger added, "It's been a huge success. We worked with the dogs in Afghanistan several times."

"We had a tracking system for those dogs that left the military," the commander continued, "to make sure they went to good homes. But, with budget cuts, we've run into a bit of a problem."

"What problem is that?" Erick asked. "Those dogs deserve the best."

"We don't want them treated like they were in the Vietnam War," Jager said, his voice hard.

"Absolutely," the commander said. "I've got a dozen K9 files here of dogs that have ended their naval careers. However, we've lost track of them. The cases were supposed to be looked into, as we want to make sure our veterans, human and K9, are well cared for. But so much work is involved, and we're constantly dealing with other aspects of the K9 program, so we have no time to investigate. I find that very difficult, and I can't ignore these dogs' plights."

"What situations are they in now?"

"Everything," the commander said. "You know we have a system for naming them, and all these dogs are tattooed in a specific sequence. I have the fact sheets in each of their files. For example, the first one graduated and was immediately sent to Afghanistan. He was active for about nine months. His owner took an IED and went home as a quadriplegic. The dog went home with him, not as injured but as no longer fit for active duty. Unfortunately the owner was involved in a severe crash within six months of getting home and was killed. His wife couldn't handle the situation, and the dog was handed over to a dog trainer, who then found a home for him, who then got rid of the dog because he had behavioral problems. And so on. His whereabouts are now unknown."

The men exchanged hard glances.

"What is it you would like us to do?" Cade asked cautiously.

"I deeply care about these animals that have served our country," the commander said in a low voice, "so I'm asking you to do anything you can to locate them, to ensure they are in a good environment. But only if you can volunteer your time because there's zero budget money. Otherwise I'd be getting my men here to do this."

"You want us to track down the dogs and make sure they are okay?" Badger asked.

"We created these dogs," the commander said. "We made them the trained soldiers they are. Society seems to think, if these K9s can't get along with people, then the only answer is to put them down. But if there is *any other* answer, I would like to think we would take that avenue first."

The men looked at each other again.

Jager said, "I'm game."

Geir nodded. "Always. One of those dogs took an IED for me over in Afghanistan. Blew up his trainer too. Those animals deserve the best care that we can possibly give them."

"And, for these twelve animals, we have failed them," the commander said. "I'm not assigning blame, and I can't accept the guilt, but, as a country, we have failed these animals. I'm asking you to find it in your hearts to help them."

"Any suggestions on how?" Laszlo asked. "We're hardly

flush with funds ourselves."

"Understood," the commander returned. "That's why I delayed contacting you. I can't pay you, but … if you ever need anything else …"

Badger smiled. Having the help of a commander was priceless. He glanced around at the others. They were all grinning. "We'll find a way," Badger said. "No promises on the time frame."

"Perfect," the commander said. "Faxing the files to you now as we speak."

The whirring of the fax machine in Badger's office confirmed the commander's words.

"As for suggestions on how to find them, … everything we have is in each of the files. Go carefully. Make sure they don't need anything. That they're safe. That the people around them are too."

The men nodded.

"That's a problem with people and dogs normally," Badger said. "And trained dogs no longer working with their trained handlers get confused and frustrated at the lack of commands—often becoming dangerous."

"Exactly," the commander said. "I don't have anybody else to dump this special project on. And I'm sorry. It really is a dump. It's only because I care that I'm even contacting you. If you get any good results, I'd love to hear back. You're my last hope." And he hung up.

Badger lifted a single sheet of paper in his hand, the topmost from the fax machine, still printing out more. "He's sending me all the files for the twelve dogs listed here."

"That's a brutal change for these animals," Geir said. "Those dogs are incredibly well-trained and thrive within that structured environment."

"They were also extremely attached to their handlers, and the bond is mutual, like any pet owner," Jager said. "So where are the trainers and handlers who worked with these animals? Isn't that the first and foremost responsibility of these initial specialists assigned to the K9s, as in most cases they become the owners after the dogs are discharged?"

"Yes, and no," Badger said. "You heard what the commander said regarding this first case. We've got a handler-turned-owner who came home already severely handicapped and then died. When you think about it, his civilian wife can't handle that service dog, particularly if it's new to her family, not to mention when dealing with her own personal loss. She's also moved now and apparently doesn't know who the trainer pawned the dog off on, as she was only too happy to get rid of a *problem*."

"Exactly, although finding where the dog is now could be a dead end," Geir said. "But I'm all for trying."

"Let's get a show of hands."

Unanimously all seven raised their hands.

Badger nodded. "That's why the commander asked us. We're very much like those dogs. We were also lost in many ways. And we've picked ourselves up and pulled together as a team. We are who we are because of each other. It's up to us to find these dogs and to make sure they are okay."

Geir said, "But none of us have K9 training."

"True," Badger said. "What about asking some of the men who work for us now? Find out who of them might have K9 training and go from there."

"Ethan," Jager said. "He's swinging a hammer on Geir's house. He's an electrician by trade in the military, a very handy guy to have around. A little bit of a loner, like the rest of us, but he moved to the K9 Unit eight or so years ago and served in that capacity in Afghanistan."

"Ethan? He was K9?" Cade asked. "I didn't know that."

"That's right. I heard something about that." Geir's fingers thrummed the table in front of him. "He's also a hell of a worker."

"Yes, he is. I've spoken to him about what happened in Afghanistan. He doesn't say much, but I gather the same accident that took his dog also took his leg," Jager said. "I highly suggest we talk to him first, see if he's willing to take the first dog file."

"The first file?" Erick asked in surprise. "Are you thinking of asking a different man to look at each file?"

"Why don't we start with Ethan? Maybe he can run this whole K9 locate-and-update division. Or at least give us some leads on other K9 personnel. It's possible Ethan knows men in the industry who are back home again who can take this on," Talon said, speaking up for the first time. "Ethan needs a purpose in his life anyway. But we can't discount the idea that these dogs could be all across the country and beyond."

"It wouldn't hurt to talk to him," Badger said with a nod. "I think he's the right man, but Ethan has to be willing."

"That's good enough for me," Laszlo said. "I like the idea of Ethan handling this completely, whether he's hands-on for each lost K9 or just managing any other men assigned to these files as needed."

Erik nodded. "Ethan is a good man. Although he's not easy to talk to. A loner by nature. And he is lost. I think what's lost is that missing K9 partner in his life. Once you're part of a K9 Unit, it's pretty hard to walk away from it." He paused, his gaze going from one to the other. "What about money though? Are we offering any? Not that we have to offer ..."

"I suggest we call Ethan in the morning," Badger stated, "put the proposition before him and see what his response is."

"How about we don't give him a whole lot of choices?" Jager said. "Like most of us, he has learned to take orders and to follow directions. I say we tell him that we're looking for a dog, give him an overview, then ask him to go after it."

"Maybe during his free time. He has to make money too."

The others all agreed.

Badger smiled. "Ethan's better off financially than most, after inheriting his grandparents' estate. So that might not be as big of an issue as we're thinking. Plus this might bring back his passion for life again."

"It's all about how we approach it," Erick said with a grin. "As we well know with the women, it's all in how everything is approached." He smiled down at his wedding ring as he turned it on his finger. "Just like they surprised us, I suggest we surprise Ethan. We all know it's what he really wants to do."

"It's possible." Jager nodded. "But again, it has to be his decision."

"Agreed." Badger raised an eyebrow, looking around as everybody nodded. "Agreed by all then. Ethan is it." He picked up the topmost pages from the fax machine and laughed. "Even better, this dog was lost in Texas. Last known location was Houston."

"Perfect." Cade laughed. "At least he'd have some support there with Levi and his teams nearby."

Badger's phone rang. He picked it up and chuckled.

"Guess who? Perfect timing. Let's talk to him right now."

CHAPTER 1

ETHAN NEBBERLY STUDIED the desolate ground ahead of him. His gaze shifted slowly, looking for any sign of movement. He'd caught sight of a dog from the corner of his eye as he drove past. He'd turned around and gone back. He didn't have any business taking this detour, but, seeing the injured shepherd take off, away from him, his only thought had been to help.

Ever since Badger had talked to Ethan, he'd been hard-pressed to think of anything but finding the dog in the K9:01 file. Ethan was never one to leave an animal in need and wanted to get started right away. Badger had persuaded him to slow down and to give them a bit of time to gather some intel.

During training, the dog's name was Sentry, but, as he'd been handed off several times, he had likely been renamed several times. So Ethan continued to call him by a number in his head, to help distance himself from the dog's fate. The last known place for the dog was Houston, which was also convenient. Levi's Legendary Security company was in the area, close to where Ethan was now.

As soon as he realized he was heading in this direction, he'd contacted Gunner, who had been instrumental in getting Ethan into the US War Dogs Association program years ago. They'd kept in touch ever since. Gunner had never been one to leave an animal in need either and couldn't wait for Ethan to "get his ass over" to his place, as he had put it.

There. Out of the corner of Ethan's eye again, he sensed movement. The small shepherd lay still, blending in with the rock. The dog was weak enough that it couldn't keep evading Ethan. He took another step forward, hearing sounds off in the distance. But he didn't dare stop, his gaze always on the wheat-colored hide of the animal in the tall grass. Drought had taken over this area and had turned the crabgrass the same color as the dog's hair. This particular shepherd had usual dark markings up around the head and chest area but with a very light-colored back. Ethan walked several more steps, quiet in his approach.

The whisper of movement continued to his left. He did not want other people involved. He preferred to live a life on the edge of society. People asked too many questions. They assumed that politeness was friendliness, and then they dug into Ethan's life, well past the point he was prepared to share anything.

This dog called to him in a way he hadn't felt since his military K9 days. He'd seen more than his fair share of injured animals, dogs hurt beyond recognition, where a bullet had been a mercy killing. But then he'd seen men in the same condition too.

Sometimes he wondered if those people would have preferred a bullet, just like those dogs he'd worked with. Ethan himself was one of the walking wounded. He understood some of what this dog was going through. Another step and the shepherd locked its gaze on him. From the dog's size, he'd guess she was a young female. She was exhausted, angry, hurt and incredibly dangerous. A low growl erupted from the back of the dog's throat.

Ethan stilled, sending waves of loving energy toward the animal. He didn't know if it helped, but he'd always had a way with dogs, particularly the vicious ones. Then he'd rather spend his time with four-legged animals than the two-legged ones.

He'd spent a lifetime hunting down the two-legged ones. Hunting this four-legged one was out of compassion; Ethan couldn't walk away and leave it alone.

Behind him, a man called out, "Hey, can I help you?"

Ethan didn't answer. He knew that was the starting volley. More questions would follow.

He took another step toward the shepherd. The growl picked up again; this time he knew the other man could hear it too. His footsteps stopped, but Ethan didn't let his gaze slide. He crouched slowly, and the shepherd's muted growl descended an octave, but it didn't stop.

He never said a word to the animal. The animal already knew words were false. She'd heard them before. No way the injury she sported was anything but man-made. Ethan crouched lower, taking another step toward the dog.

Behind Ethan came soft running footsteps, but again he didn't dare take a chance to look. He held up a palm toward whoever approached. The footsteps stopped again. When Ethan caught the sucked-in breath of the man closing in on him, he knew he too had seen the shepherd.

The shepherd started to growl again.

"Are you sure you want to approach her?" the stranger asked softly.

Ethan gave a single head nod, keeping his hand up to stop the man from approaching. Ethan took another step, crouching even lower to appear less threatening to the injured animal.

And then again, maybe not to this poor animal, having suffered abuse at the hands of a human.

Ethan could sympathize with that mentality. It wasn't that he was antisocial, but he was antipeople. Still, he'd agreed to see Gunner, and he was on the hunt for a missing dog. Not this one unfortunately. Ethan was after a big male with different coloring.

He took two more steps toward the shepherd; her eyes had a dull glaze in them, as if she had no more fight left in her. He was only three feet away. He dropped to his knees and just sat here, studying her injuries. Blood was on her flank; her leg had an open wound—showing tendon, muscle, possibly bone—but also her front shoulder needed to be looked at closer. She was starving, on the run and hurting. She'd made her last stand, and she figured she was done.

He reached out a hand in a nonthreatening way, lowered himself farther to the ground. Her eyes tracked him, but she never made a sound. Her eyes were golden and filmed with pain but still with enough fire to cause him serious injury if she went for him. Though he was concerned about her and her injuries, he had to convince her of that. Only silence floated on the wind behind him. The grass gently wafted to the side as a breeze rolled over them, and none of it mattered to her.

Or to him.

He took another slow, cautious shuffle forward. Her muscles bunched, the corner of her lips pulled back, showing her teeth, but no heat accompanied the sound coming from her throat. He slipped closer. And then she did something that made his heart break.

She just lay her head down and gave up.

He hated to see that because he'd been there himself.

Tears burned the corners of his eyes as he watched one of the proudest, strongest, most beautiful animals in the world just roll over and say, *I'm done.* That was *so* not helping right now. He needed her to fight what was coming. It would be ugly, but, if he could coax her through it, she'd be fine on the other side. But the next hour, the next day, maybe the next several weeks, if not months, would be a painful recovery. It would be a bitch.

But, with his help, she could master her recovery.

He gently reached out a hand toward her fur.

The stranger behind him murmured, "Careful. She's not totally done yet. There's still fire in her eye."

Ethan gave a clipped nod because *that* was a good thing. Maybe she hadn't totally given up. He laid a hand on her shoulder, feeling her tremble underneath his hand, her body shaking with fear. But she was so weak, she could do nothing more than lie here, knowing the end was coming. He ran a quick hand down her back, feeling each and every rib. Her leg was broken, the skin open and crusty with infection. She had wounds on her belly, and he just wasn't sure what else.

"Was she hit by a car?" asked the man, now beside him.

Ethan nodded.

"I have an anesthetic in my hand. I'd like to administer it to the shepherd, so we can get her some help."

Slowly Ethan raised his head from the animal in front of him and took a calculated risk to turn to look at the big man at his side. He studied the bald head, the massive shoulders of a man in a muscle shirt and shorts, with a very interesting prosthetic at the end of a stump barely showing underneath the tied-up shorts. *Stone.* He held out a syringe.

"Hello, Stone. I'll take it."

Stone nodded, and the syringe slowly crossed hands. The

shepherd, her body shaking, watched, the whites of her eyes showing.

With a gentle hand Ethan slowly administered the anesthetic to take the dog's pain several levels down. He doubted it was enough to knock her out, but, if it was enough to move her, at least they could get her some help.

"A vet's around the corner," Stone said. "An animal rescue's just down the hill."

Ethan's gaze narrowed as he studied his surroundings. He hadn't realized he was so close to Anna and Flynn's place. He waited for the anesthesia to take effect and for the shepherd's eyes to slowly close. He handed the syringe back to Stone as he slowly straightened. "Kat says hi."

Stone's eyes widened, and the corner of his mouth kicked up. "Well, I'll be damned. Ethan. It is you. I wasn't sure initially, but there aren't too many humans I know who can approach a wounded animal like you just did."

Ethan's lips twitched at that response. "Not quite as smooth or as good as I used to be." He motioned to Stone's leg. "I think I'm wearing a more advanced model than you are."

Stone blustered. "No way. How could Kat not give me the latest and the best?" he asked with a huge grin. He reached out a hand and shook Ethan's. "Damn, you're a sight for sore eyes. It's been what? Three or four years since I saw you last?"

Ethan shrugged. "Maybe. It's been half that long since I was in active service."

"Levi said something about you coming but didn't expect you so soon. Neither did I hear much about the reason why you're here. Other than meeting up with Gunner."

"I'm following up on a request from up the chain of

command. Looking for a K9 dog that might or might not be okay. And, yep, Gunner is on my list of people to stop by and see."

"Gunner is a good guy. I know he's looking for a pair of security dogs. Sounds like you two should do well." Stone pointed down the hill. "I was helping out at Anna's place, building another set of dog runs, when I saw you up here." His gaze dropped to Ethan's legs. "Sorry about the accident that took your leg. Sometimes life's a bitch, isn't it?"

Ethan dropped his gaze to the dog at his feet. "And sometimes it's the bitches that are life." He turned to look at his truck parked on the side of the highway. "I don't know how badly hurt she is, but it looks bad."

"Louise will let us know," Stone said.

Ethan walked around and gently scooped his hands underneath the frail dog. He motioned toward his truck. "I can hold her, if you can drive."

Surprise lit Stone's gaze again. He judged the distance and said, "You'll ride in the bed or in the front?"

"In the bed."

Stone nodded once, and the two men, not saying another word, strode over to Ethan's big black Dodge Ram 3500 pickup. It took a little bit of scrambling to get into the bed of the truck, while holding the shepherd, but Ethan managed it.

"Nice wheels," Stone said as he shut the tailgate and then hopped into the driver's side and turned the key, starting the engine. With Stone driving carefully, they headed down the road.

In the distance Ethan could see other people watching the two of them. He ignored them, keeping his focus on the shepherd in his arms. He shifted her weight and caught sight of the tattoo number on her leg. Not a navy number but from a breeder or the owner. She could have a chip too. He'd need a vet to look for that. He noted it. Someone had cared about her once.

He'd find out soon enough.

Not even ten minutes later they pulled into a large parking lot to an even larger animal clinic. Stone hopped out, came around and opened the tailgate, so Ethan could slide out with his precious cargo. Then they walked inside.

By the time Ethan made it through the double glass doors, a gurney was already pushed toward him. Very gently he laid the shepherd on it.

A woman stepped in front of him, took one look at the shepherd and said, "Do you know what happened?"

Ethan shook his head. "I saw her an hour or so ago. I've been tracking her since."

Stone interrupted. "Louise, this is the shepherd we told you about. The one we couldn't get close to."

Her gaze went from one man to the other; then she looked at the shepherd. "Well, somebody managed to." She turned, pushing the gurney toward the internal set of opaque doors, marked Surgery. "I'll let you know what I find."

Ethan followed.

She stopped at the surgery doors and faced him, shaking her head. "Medical personnel only."

He crossed his arms over his chest and glared at her.

She hesitated, looked at Stone, then back at Ethan. "So you're one of them?"

He raised one eyebrow.

She sighed. "Do you have any training?"

He tilted his head to the side. "Field style."

She groaned. "Of course you do. You're a handler."

He gave a slight shrug. "You could say that. Trainer, handler, keeper of War Dogs."

She looked torn.

"I want to remain beside her."

Louise made a quick decision and gave him a clipped nod. "Stay out of my way."

He didn't answer, just placed a hand on the shepherd and followed alongside the gurney. He walked into a large room with multiple surgical areas.

Louise snapped out orders. Staff came from several corners, and, while Ethan watched, blood was taken, X-rays were snapped, and a full physical exam was done, quickly but efficiently.

Louise said finally, "I'll be back in a minute. I want to see her X-rays."

Ethan hadn't said a word, his hand on the shepherd's head, gently stroking it to let her know she wasn't alone.

Finally Louise came back. "She's in pretty rough shape." She then ordered IVs for the dog. "We'll get some fluids and some nutrients into her and try to stabilize her. She's got a couple busted ribs. Her leg is broken. The back leg looks to have taken a severe blow. We might have to put pins in her hip," she admitted cautiously. "Someone shot her as well, a glancing blow off the right shoulder. But her broken leg, I can't say that it's looking terribly positive." She pulled her phone out and brought up a photo.

Ethan's heart sunk at the news.

"You aren't her owner. So who will pay for this?" she asked.

"I will."

Surprise lit her eyes. "Glad to hear that. Will you let us look after her?"

He patted and studied the soft fur on the dog's head. "Yes. I think her hip is okay though. It won't need pins."

"I'll see as I get further along. It looks like the animal is young and in emaciated condition when she was hit. Probably dragged herself off the road and has been trying to survive ever since."

He nodded. "Fix her up." He took a step back. "No matter the cost."

Louise hesitated, then said softly, "You know it could be expensive."

"I can easily make more money." His gaze was steady, and then he nodded. "Sometimes we all need something more than merely money." On those words, he turned and walked out of the surgery room. Instinctively he knew Louise was one of the vets who cared. And she'd do everything she could to keep that shepherd alive.

CINNAMON MICHELSON STUDIED the man standing at the surgery doors, his hands shoved deep into his pockets, a grim line on his lips, his jaw clenched. She didn't understand what was going on, but whatever it was hurt him. Even as she watched, a muscle in his jaw flexed at something happening on the other side of the frosted glass.

He stayed there for too long. She didn't think it could be good for him. Obviously an injured animal was in there, and it was one he cared about deeply. She'd brought in a friend's dog for more of a grooming-related visit, one she looked after on a regular basis. The little guy would be another half hour yet before he would be ready to go home.

She turned to look around the large sitting room, then

walked to the coffeepot. There she poured two cups. She looked at the man still standing at the door and headed to him. "I thought you could use this."

He turned to look at her with a speed that almost made her spill the coffee. Instantly his hands reached out and studied her, but he didn't grab the hot cups. He had grabbed her wrists.

Her breath released slowly. In a gentle voice she said, "I'm sorry. I didn't mean to startle you. I brought you a cup of coffee."

At the confusion in his eyes and the intent way he looked at her, she had to wonder how long it had been since anybody had done such a simple deed for him.

She smiled up at him. "You didn't look like the kind of guy who would use sugar."

He tilted his head to the side, looked down at her wrists. He dropped her hands and accepted the cup. In a low, deep voice, he said, "Thank you. And, no, no sugar."

She motioned toward the area where the coffee was set up and said, "If you need creamer, it's over there."

His lips quirked. "Black is the only way to drink coffee." He glanced at his cup and over at hers, then said, "Thank you. I'm sorry for grabbing you."

His voice seemed almost … rusty, as if maybe the apology or the polite conversation was hard for him.

She didn't know what it was about these injured animals, but she was a sucker for each and every one. She tilted her head in a gentle motion, wary of making a faster motion and scaring him. "You didn't hurt me, so it's all right." She stepped back and sat in one of the chairs against the wall. "It doesn't help to stand there and watch the animals on the other side. You know that, right?"

His eyes shuttered away something, like he took a step backward into his own little world again. She was sorry she'd brought it up.

He gave her a crooked smile and said, "Nothing wrong with doing it either."

"Don't you think it hurts you more?" she asked. "Whatever injured animal is in there is getting the best help they can get. Louise is phenomenal."

"I don't know her," he said, "but I'm hoping that shepherd gets the care she needs."

"Is she yours?"

A second curtain went down, shielding whatever else his eyes might reveal. He gave a brief shake of his head. "No, I saw her when I drove past the road. Then stopped to help her."

"Any idea what happened?" she asked curiously. She hadn't told him that most of what she did was arrange for animal adoptions, usually from other countries, but sometimes within the general area or across the country. She and Anna worked closely together. He probably didn't know Anna and probably didn't know about Anna's shelter.

"No," he said, his voice tight. "Possibly hit by a vehicle."

She felt herself recoil against that. "An all-too-common occurrence," she murmured. She dropped her gaze to the cup of coffee in her hand and lifted it, hoping it wouldn't burn her lips. She blew over the cup's edge, and, when she thought it was safe, she took a sip. "What are you doing after she's taken care of?"

He only looked at her.

"Or have you not thought that far ahead?"

He raised his gaze. "I'm not sure," he admitted. "But I couldn't leave her out there."

Cinn's heart melted a little. Any guy who would go to this much effort to save an injured shepherd couldn't be bad. Those who looked after animals the best were usually injured in some way themselves. Maybe in the hopes somebody would treat them better too. In a moment of self-clarity, she thought, *I have to stop psychoanalyzing men.* It had gotten her into trouble more than a few times. On dogs, that worked great. But men were a different story.

"Anna and Flynn's shelter is around the corner," Cinn said gently. "They might take her in."

He shook his head. "No. I'm not deserting her."

A wealth of emotion was in that word *deserting*. She sat quietly contemplating what that meant to a man who appeared to be lost in his own world.

"*Can* you look after her?" she asked suddenly, worried the shepherd would end up in a situation worse than the one this man had found her in.

"Yes."

And that was all he said. She didn't have any right to push it. But it was hard not to. "I work with animal rescues around the world. We move animals into homes from country to country. If you need somebody to look after her …"

He gave a hard shake of his head but remained silent.

Even without words he had made that pretty clear. She settled in her chair and waited. Not another sound came out of him.

Finally the double doors opened, and Louise came out. She looked tired, but a happy smile appeared as she walked toward the man beside her and smiled at him. "You were right. No pins required. It was dislocated. I couldn't see that from the X-ray. Too much damage around it. I fixed her up as much as I could. She will need several days here with us."

He straightened slowly, towering over Louise. But Louise didn't appear to be intimidated in any way. Cinn wondered about that. Then again, Louise was with Rory and the rest of Levi's gang. And she was probably used to dealing with these hard alpha males. Though this one appeared to be a broken, dangerous one.

Cinn sighed. "I did suggest that maybe, if you didn't want to look after the shepherd, Anna might take her."

Louise turned and looked at Cinn with a smile. "Hey. I didn't see you there. You've been talking to this gentleman, have you?"

Cinn nodded. But the man in question never moved.

"Stone said your name is Ethan?" Louise asked boldly.

Ethan gave a clipped nod.

"Do you live around here?"

Ethan shrugged.

Louise appeared satisfied with that.

But, for Cinn, it raised a million more questions. Stone knew him? She knew Stone from Anna and Flynn's place. Many of Levi's men came to help out there. But she'd never seen Ethan before. Who was he? Where was he staying? She thought she knew every local male. And what kind of a man went out of his way to help a shepherd and to stay to hear her prognosis? The shepherd would need long-term care until she was fully healed. Was he ready for that?

"I want to see her," Ethan said.

Louise considered him for a long moment. "When we get her set up in the cage, I'll let you in for a minute."

The briefest of smiles crossed his face, but it was enchanting to Cinn. He sat abruptly, taking a sip of his coffee.

Louise headed back into the surgery area. Knowing the

way she worked, chances were she would deal with another half-dozen animals before her day was done.

Cinn had often wondered about getting more education, but just the thought of seven years of vet school had been enough to stop her. She was a project manager, a job she operated from home for a large company. It gave her a lot of freedom, so she could continue her volunteer work with the animals. Though sometimes it was difficult to make both of them work.

Just then Megan, the receptionist, called Cinn's name. Cinn walked over to see Mitzi, the little shih tzu she'd brought in for her friend Sandra, being led toward her.

"Her nails are taken care of," Megan said. "That one toenail was infected, but we've cleaned it out, disinfected it, and she should be good to go now."

Chuckling at the greeting Mitzi gave her, Cinn bent down, scooped her into her arms and said, "Are you okay to put this on Sandra's account, or do you want me to cover it?"

"It's all good," Megan said.

Cinn waved goodbye and left her empty coffee cup on the counter where she'd placed it. At her car, she put Mitzi into the carrier in the back, snapped it tight, making sure the seat belt was buckled, and got into the front seat.

As she looked up, she saw Ethan sitting where she'd left him, looking at her. She glanced around and saw the big black truck and knew instinctively it would be his. She frowned, wondering what she should do and why she wasn't pulling away. Because she sure as hell should be. Finally she reached for her notebook and, wondering if this was a mistake, wrote down her name, phone number and a brief note underneath. She pulled the sheet of paper from the notebook, exited the car, walked over to the truck and tucked it under his wipers. She got back into her car and drove away.

She saw black clouds forming above, and she mentally told Ethan to hurry and read her note because the rain would smear the ink. She figured what she had done was very stupid, but she couldn't help herself. That man looked like he needed a friend.

CHAPTER 2

A FTER DELIVERING MITZI to her very grateful owner—a mother with a newborn demanding most of her attention—Cinn returned to her home. She was behind on her own personal work, and then there was always the inevitable volunteer work. She parked her SUV in the driveway, got out and heard her dogs barking in the backyard. Instead of going to the front door, she walked through the gate around to the side yard, watching the dogs bound toward her. One was a basset hound missing a leg; another was a lab that thought everybody was his best friend. The two dogs got along well together and with the spares she brought home.

She bent over, giving them both a greeting. "Hey, I was only gone for a couple hours, guys. It was all good."

They kept pace with her as she walked to the back of the house and into the kitchen. There she dumped her purse and walked over to the stove, putting on the teakettle. It was a beautiful September day. She loved fall, and, once temperatures calmed down a bit, then she would be outside every day, all day. But, for now, she had to provide a living for herself and her furry family.

After making a sandwich, she took it and her cup of tea into her home office and sat down before her computer. She opened her work email and groaned when she saw twenty-

one new messages had dropped into her in-box. But this was
what she did, and the paycheck was very decent. She didn't
have any right to complain.

Several hours later, the dogs crazily barking had startled
her out of her reverie. As the dogs reached the front door,
they both fell silent and sat just inside the door, tails wagging. She studied them. Looking through the nearby window
at the shadow outside the door, she knew who it was.
Hesitatingly, wondering why the hell she was even thinking
of doing this, she left the chain on the door and opened it
the little bit the chain allowed. "Hello?"

He stared at her, his chin dropping and his eyebrows
rising.

She looked at him nonplussed. That she was correct
about him being behind her door wasn't necessarily good.
Still, she'd left that note because she wanted to see him. But
the note didn't have her address on it. "How did you know
where I live?"

"The clinic."

She shook her head. "No, they wouldn't have shared
that personal information."

He pulled out his phone and showed her a page he had
been on. It was her license plate with her address.

"Now that makes sense," she said on a sigh. "Not too
many people know how to pull up an address off a license
plate."

"Let's just say, I know some people," he said smoothly.

"Levi? Stone? Flynn?"

He nodded.

"But you don't work for them?" She bit her lower lip, as
she tried to figure out what to do about this. "Then why lie
to me?"

"Most women would be uncomfortable with this method, so I thought saying the clinic told me would be easier."

She had given him her name and number in her note, but he hadn't followed up on that by calling. He'd taken a different route.

"I'm making you uncomfortable," he said in that low voice. "I'll leave." He turned to walk back down the front steps.

Immediately she took off the chain and pulled open the door, still not leaving her house. "Wait."

On the bottom step he turned and looked at her. "You shouldn't have opened the door to a stranger."

She raised both hands. "Yeah, I've heard that before too."

He looked at her steadily. "You can call Stone, if you know him."

She grabbed her phone and called Levi's compound. "Hey, Ice. Is Stone there?"

Ice laughed and said, "I think he just came in. Hang on."

Within minutes Stone's heavy, deep voice came into her ear, "What's up, Cinn?"

"Do you know Ethan?"

Stone sucked in breath on the other end, and he answered cautiously, "If you mean the Ethan who picked up the shepherd this morning, yes, I know him. We have friends in common."

"What friends?" she demanded.

"They're in the next state over," he said slowly. "Another group of friends of ours. Ethan's okay. He's been through a lot though."

"But you can vouch for him?"

"I can vouch he's honorable, and he's damaged, and that shepherd was very important to him."

"Well, those three things I could figure out myself," she said in exasperation. "But thanks." She hung up the phone, pocketed it, knowing, if anything happened to her, Stone would know who was responsible. She threw the door open wide for him to enter. "Come on in."

The dogs happily exited the house, greeting him as a long-lost friend.

He stood on the porch for a long moment, petting the animals. "Stone knows me but not well."

She nodded. "He said as much. He also said you're honorable but damaged."

Ethan lifted a pant leg and showed her what appeared to be a prosthetic limb.

She nodded. "That explains the gait."

"What gait?"

"You went down the stairs stiffly," she answered, walking toward her kitchen. "I'll put on coffee. Do you want a cup?"

He leaned against the entranceway to the kitchen, a safe distance away, as if giving her space. "Thank you. I'd appreciate it."

She silently put on a small pot, then felt awkward as she searched for a topic of conversation. "What's the state of the shepherd?"

"She's doing much better."

"Is she awake from the anesthesia yet?"

He gave her a glimmer of a smile and shook his head. "But she's resting easier. More at peace."

She thought about that and nodded. "I guess that's fair. Sometimes animals don't rest, even when they are under anesthesia, do they? It's more of a forced rest. But, if she's looking better, that's good."

He sat at the kitchen table, choosing the chair closest to him.

She said, "Or we can sit outside on the deck."

He stood again in a smooth motion and waited. Always silent, mostly still. She poured coffee in two cups, leading the way to the large veranda that ran along the back of her house. The dogs raced out into the backyard. A ball sat beside one of the patio chairs. With the coffee cups still in her hand, she kicked the ball across the yard. Both dogs tumbled after it. She placed the coffee cups on the patio table and took a seat. The dogs came back with the ball, eager for more. She grinned to see Burglar had won.

"You have a three-legged basset hound?"

She nodded. "Got him from Anna. His name is Burglar. He was trying to steal something from a butcher shop when the door closed on his leg, one with automatic locks, and it wouldn't open again. He lost circulation, and the leg had to be removed." Out of the corner of her eye, she watched a smile whisper across his face. "You really like animals, don't you?"

He nodded. "They're simple, straightforward, honest, clear-cut. They don't play sneaky mind games."

"Unlike humans, you mean?"

Again he nodded. He reached down, and Burglar dropped the ball into his hand. Ethan tossed it high and long into the yard. Both dogs raced after it. "What's the Lab's name?"

"Midnight," she said. "She was another foster dog of Anna's. She's way too friendly with everybody, so, the minute she escapes a fenced-in yard, she's gone looking for the next person who will give her attention."

"Do you have a securely fenced yard?" he asked, his gaze looking around the property.

"Several of them," she admitted. "I have a lot of dog runs here. Depending on what animals we're moving, if I have to get involved personally. I have ten acres here."

Appreciation lit his gaze. "I really like that idea. I'm not much for town living."

"Neither am I," she said. "Stone said something about you having mutual friends in another state."

He gave her a crooked smile. "That's true. In New Mexico—Santa Fe. Badger was in one of my units way back. And I served with Stone. But not the same unit. That was a few years ago."

"That explains the look to you," she said. "You and Stone both have that hard edge that says life hasn't been easy."

"Is life meant to be easy?" he asked with interest.

"I don't know," she admitted. "But I sure wouldn't mind if it was."

He just smiled and didn't say anything.

"So, if you're not from around here, what's the plan when the shepherd's able to move?"

"Are you worried about me or worried about the shepherd?"

"Both," she said shortly. "You both look broken."

He stared at her steadfastly, his eyes almost dark, like Midnight's, her Lab. He said in a calm, quiet voice, "I was broken. But I've put myself back together again. The shepherd will need help to do that. I hope to provide it for her."

"Any idea what happened to her?"

He shook his head, then studied her for a long moment, reached into his jeans pocket and pulled out something. He placed it on the small table in front of her.

A smashed metal piece.

She frowned at it, her throat tightening. "Somebody shot her?" She stared at him in horror, and then a realization dawned. "After she got hit by the vehicle, right? To put her out of her misery because she was so badly injured?"

He shook his head. "No. I think she was shot, was on the run, then was hit. She was very emaciated. Then she ran into traffic."

Inside, Cinn's stomach churned. "I hope not. I hate when animals get hurt unnecessarily. Animal cruelty will never sit well with me."

Just then Burglar ran toward her with the ball. She smiled, reached down, scrubbed his long ears and neck, took the ball and threw it again for him.

"Everyone here carries guns," Ethan said. "Do you know anybody who would have shot the shepherd?"

She shook her head. "No."

"How about anybody who's working with drugs?"

She frowned at him, not sure where this was going. "Well, I don't do drugs, and I don't know anybody who's involved in the drug trade, if that's what you're asking."

He nodded but stared out at the world around him, not really seeing it.

"Why do you ask?" she asked.

"Because I think she was a highly trained dog."

"*Highly trained*? Like, a police dog? A drug-sniffing dog?"

He nodded. "I think so."

"How can you tell?"

"She's tattooed, for one. I already traced it. She was police trained, but that ID isn't active. So either she didn't make the grade or was trained for something nonmilitary."

"They have a database for that?"

"If you know where to look," he said absentmindedly.

"She's lucky you found her," she said. "I hope you keep her and nurse her back to full health."

"We will," he murmured.

"*We?*"

Surprised, he gave himself almost a mental headshake and turned to look at her. "I meant, she and I will."

"Are you working?" she asked.

"You ask a lot of questions," he countered.

She sighed. "I asked because of Levi's crew around the corner. It seems he's always bringing in new men."

He shrugged. "I don't plan on working for Levi. But the opportunity is there, if I want to."

"It still doesn't make any sense that a dog would have been around drugs, get shot, hit by a vehicle, and then left to die," she cried out. "Who does that?"

He slowly turned to look at her, and the smile on his face sent chills down her spine. "I don't know who does that," he said in that voice so soft, and yet, so chilling with purpose, "yet." Then he added, "But they won't do it a second time."

"LOUISE REMOVED THE bullet that had ripped through the back of the dog's shoulder, thankfully, instead of her chest," Ethan said, "but she was so emaciated." He shook his head. "As if she'd been kept captive, starving for a long time."

"Well, I'm glad she's free then," Cinn said. "But you can't just go after whoever did this."

He looked at her steadily.

She knew that expression and sighed deeply. "If they shot the dog, what are the chances they'll shoot you, if you stick your nose in their business?"

This time he grinned, showing teeth.

She sat back. "You're going after them because of what they did to her, aren't you?"

"If you could, wouldn't you?" he asked. "Besides, if there is one abused shepherd there, maybe there are more." He sat up taller. "The reason I came here was to track down a big male shepherd cross, part of the military War Dogs unit." He explained what happened to the dog. "Making sure he's okay. It's quite possible that he is at the same place where the female came from."

Cinn's face scrunched up, making her prominent freckles come close together, giving a shadow to her cheekbones.

He didn't think he'd ever met anybody with as many freckles as she had. It was a cute look, and she seemed to come from the heart.

"Wow. I had no idea anyone cared about those K9 dogs after they were done in the military. But I'm very happy to hear they are looked after. And, yes," she said. "Many times I wished I had the means to go after some of these assholes who abuse animals. But you can't be a lone ranger. I don't know this dog you're after, but it doesn't look like you have any backup. I hate to think you're out there alone without someone to help you if things get ugly." She frowned. "And, if you're not part of Levi's crew, you're probably not protected by him or the other connections he has."

Ethan shrugged and settled back, picking up his cup of

coffee. "Doesn't matter," he said. "When you come across something that's wrong, you have to do what you can to make it right."

It was a philosophy he'd followed all his life. When he'd worked K9 Units overseas, he and his unit had been a close-knit group. Not just with the animals but with each other. He'd lost track of most of them. It crossed his mind to connect with some, but he didn't know where they were. It had also crossed his mind that Stone and maybe Levi and his group could find them, but Ethan didn't really want to spend the money on it nor did he want anybody to know what he was doing. He'd always been a private person, but, since he came out of the hospital, he'd turned hermit. Too much so.

He still couldn't understand the impulse that had led him here to Cinn's house. He'd watched her write the note and put it on his truck. Even as interest filled him, he wanted to castigate her for being such a fool to contact strange men. She couldn't know he was safe. Didn't she understand how foolish it was, how dangerous the world was? He wanted to stay and protect her from being so foolish again.

"You'll need help, if you're going after whoever shot the dog," she said. "I'm not a very brave person, but I'd do an awful lot to help save the animals."

He looked at her, not sure where this conversation was going.

"There's a property about twenty miles from here. It's a shady, ugly place, maybe twice the size my parcel is. I wouldn't be surprised if it wasn't a criminal hideout. Every time I've gone past, I see the animals there, and I put in another complaint to the city because those animals look like they're in terrible shape. But, so far, nobody's done anything.

I picked up a puppy about a mile away from there not too long ago. I didn't ask if it was theirs. The farther away I could get that puppy, the better."

"Sounds like a place to start."

She shook her head. "No, it's too far away. Your shepherd wouldn't have traveled that far."

"Dogs can do an awful lot if they are desperate."

"What purpose would that shepherd have for coming here?"

"What breed was the puppy that you picked up and how long ago?"

She looked at him in confusion. "A shepherd cross but it was six months ago I'd say. The puppy was young, maybe six weeks old at the time," she said slowly.

He nodded. "And the shepherd I found had had pups."

Her jaw dropped as he watched. "You're thinking that puppy was one of hers, and she was coming here after it?"

He shrugged. "I don't know how the time frame works, but she came here for a reason. Was the puppy staying at Anna and Flynn's place?"

She slowly nodded. "Yes. Anna took it."

"And where is it now?"

"I'd have to ask Anna. But one of Levi's crew might have adopted it. I don't know for sure."

He nodded slowly. "It would explain her need to come in this direction."

From the look on her face, she hadn't considered that, and it made her sick now. "Animals are just like people in so many ways—well, the good people," she whispered. "Steal a child from a mother, and watch her turn into a wildcat, trying to get it back again."

He nodded slowly. "People are people, and animals are

animals. Yet some instincts are universal. I can't say that's what brought the shepherd here, but I also can't say that wasn't what brought her here. She was not full of milk, so she had dried up from whatever pups she'd had, but she has given birth." He watched as she slumped in her chair and stared out at the fields around her.

"She definitely needs a chance at a better life," she murmured. "I hope she makes it."

"She'll make it," he said. But he worried too. The shepherd not only had to be strong to get through the surgery, she had to be strong to get through what it would take to get her back on her feet. "She's already been abused enough," he said. "I want to make sure that, for the rest of her natural life, she understands what love is too."

At that, Cinn shot him a sharp look. "There was a lot more human emotion in those words than I expected."

He settled back and pulled his invisible shield around him again. "I didn't mean anything by it," he said, a cool note entering his voice. "Just that the dog has had a tough life. She deserves a better one."

Cinn nodded. "But I think you've had a tough life too," she murmured. "And I think you deserve a better one as well."

He shot her a hard look. "I'm not a dog."

"No, but there are definitely similarities."

He gave a harsh laugh because she was right there. There were definite similarities. They were both junkyard dogs.

CHAPTER 3

C INN WOKE UP early and was outside in the backyard, running with the dogs as she always did. She had no style, no form. She jumped over rocks; she raced around bushes; she tossed balls for the dogs, but mostly she kept her body moving, always in a forward motion.

For some reason, Ethan slipped into her mind. He'd have a heyday with her running style. He looked like the kind who went left-right-left-right, steady for at least five miles before taking a break. Whereas she'd stop, scoop up a ball, run some more, toss the ball, keep on running, dashing around to the left, stopping to throw the dogs off the trail and then keep on going once more. She liked to have fun, and a straight jog from point A to point B wasn't enough fun for her.

The dogs stopped for a drink, while she jogged on the spot. Normally a creek flowed heavily beside her property, but it was almost dry this year. The drought had taken the creek down to just a small trickle. When she figured they'd had enough time to quench their thirst, she jumped the creek bed and carried on up the other side, the dogs at her heels. When she was about worn out, she turned and headed back toward the house. Now she'd go in a straight line home again.

By the time she hit the gate at the back of her property,

her footsteps had slowed to a walk, and she could feel her uneven breath, hot and raspy. She let herself and the dogs into the yard, walking even more slowly to the house. She had a lot of work to do today. But Ethan kept sitting in the back of her mind. She wondered what he was up to and how the shepherd was doing.

Before she realized it, her fingers dialed the clinic. They weren't open yet, but she knew Megan well and called her personal number. As soon as Megan answered, Cinn asked, "How is the shepherd doing?"

"Which one?" Megan asked in a wry tone. "This appears to be shepherd week."

Cinn chuckled. "It's so bizarre how that works."

"Hey, it's the same for all facets of life. It's like in the maternity ward. They have baby girls upon baby girls, and then, all of a sudden, it switches to baby boys."

"I meant, the shepherd Ethan brought in."

"Ah, that one," Megan said, a smile coming through the phone. "She's doing better than she deserves to be. She slept through the night. We've increased her medications for the pain, now that she's back to awareness. I expect Ethan to be on the front steps of the clinic at any moment, since we open soon."

"At least he cares."

"Right, and you can't stop thinking about him, can you?" Megan teased. "Do you want me to tell you when he gets here, so you can come around?"

"Nope. I expect he'll stop by here afterward anyway," she said. "Thanks for letting me know about the shepherd."

She hung up to avoid answering further questions and sat here for a long moment, wondering about where Ethan'd gone. But it really wasn't any of her business. It was so hard not to be curious. He was a loner, by all the things she knew about him. Everything about him made her curious. He'd arrived out of nowhere and didn't seem to have any connection to anyone or a job around here, but he knew a lot of people. She was happy he'd found the dog, or the shepherd might not have made it.

What Cinn needed to do was get back to work. She was part of a global canine rescue group. Currently they were bringing twenty dogs over from Greece. The country had hit a rough patch, and the animals, as well as the people, had suffered. The locals dumped their pets because they could no longer afford to care for them. Now starving packs of dogs ran loose in the streets, causing all kinds of mayhem.

She needed one or two shelters to take them, until they could be adopted. She was avoiding the states that had kill centers. No point in bringing a dog over here just to be killed. At the same time, she knew a lot of people were against what she was doing because so many local dogs also needed to be looked after.

That was also why she had centers in Canada and England that she worked with. Canada was always good for at least half of the animals. They had way less people but a lot more were willing to take in rescues. Considering that, she sent off an email to the three centers she worked with regularly, confirming the numbers of animals they were willing to take.

While she waited for responses, which weren't likely to come until the end of the day, she got up and made herself a shake for breakfast. She knew that Ethan's shepherd wouldn't move for quite a while, so she wondered if Ethan would stick around. Did he have a place where he could look after the dog's medical needs? She sent Louise a text, asking if the shepherd needed a home while it recovered.

Cinn could surely do something. She sent a second text, asking if Anna would be looking after the shepherd.

Surprisingly Louise answered quickly. **Ethan is taking her. But not for a few more days. She needs to be mobile and given medications.**

But that can be done at home, right?

Sure, but her bowels have to move smoothly. She doesn't leave until then.

Acknowledging that with a text back, Cinn got down to work. If Ethan would take the shepherd, that was all good.

ETHAN WAS AT the vet's office ten minutes before it opened. He got out of his vehicle, locked the truck and stood at the front door. He knew people were inside, but he didn't move from his position. They'd either let him in or not, but he wasn't budging until he had a chance to see the shepherd. He wasn't there but five more minutes when the door opened, and he saw Louise on the other side.

She smiled at him and said, "She's doing fine."

He looked at her, searching for the truth in her eyes, then asked, "May I see her?"

She nodded, let him in and then locked the door behind him.

He frowned. "Letting me in is not a good practice."

She chuckled. "Now you sound like my partner and the rest of the gang in my life."

"Who's your partner?" he asked, curious if he knew him.

"Rory. He works for Levi."

Ethan nodded. He knew many of Levi's men but not

Rory in particular.

"Are you working for Levi too?"

"I don't think so," Ethan said. "I'm not sure what I'm doing at the moment." It was the truth but sounded worse when spoken out loud. "I am on an assignment for someone else at the moment."

"Ah," Louise said with a smile. "I think all the men who work for Levi worked for someone else."

Not sure what to say to that, Ethan said nothing and followed her through to the surgery room and beyond. He studied the gleaming surgical tables, rows of instruments, cupboards, panels of parts used in surgery. They walked to a wall of cages. There were cats, dogs, bunnies, and he was surprised to see a ferret.

"She's down here," Louise said. She crouched in front of a large dog crate that had a name tag and a clipboard attached with the details of the animal inside. She opened the front so he could see the shepherd huddled in the back.

He crouched in front of her. The dog whined as in recognition. He reached out a hand and laid it on her forehead calmly. The shepherd didn't move; her eyes were glazed with pain. Louise checked her over while he gave her what comfort he could. "Any idea how long she'll be here?"

"A couple days," Louise said. "I need to make sure that she can walk and that her bodily functions work properly. And we have to confirm she's not bleeding anymore. I won't be happy until I can see her walking around the parking lot on her own steam. Animals heal much faster than people do."

"Humans make healing hard work." He could feel her odd look at his comment, but he meant it. Animals were simple. When they needed care, or they needed food, they were happy to get it. He gently stroked between the shepherd's eyes, his fingers soft, comforting.

"She recognizes you," Louise commented. "Accepts you."

"I didn't hurt her," he said. "That already marks me as one of the good guys." He heard Louise's heavy sigh.

"Unfortunately you're quite right there. Do you have much history on her?"

"Not yet," he said, stroking the soft ears as she lay here with her eyes closed, allowing him to touch her. "But I will."

"Without getting hurt yourself, I hope," she said, her tone sharp.

His only response was to stare at her.

She sighed. "No point in talking to you on this issue, is there?"

"Any point in talking to Rory or Stone or any of the other men?"

She chuckled. "No. Not about stuff like this." She straightened. "If you'd like, you can sit here. But I can't move her, so please only touch her head and keep her calm. My assistant will come in and change her dressings again later."

He nodded. "I'll stay with her for a few minutes."

Louise nodded and checked on several other animals while he watched with interest.

He dropped his gaze to the shepherd. She had her eyes closed, relaxing. His fingers stroked down her nose and back up between her eyes and over to gently caress her long silky ears. "What happened to you, girl?" he asked softly.

Her ears twitched at his tone of voice, so he kept talking to her gently, if for nothing else than to get her to remember his voice. That would be huge. Speaking calmly, he told her that he would look after her and that the worst of her life was over. But she had to heal, she had to fight and get back up on her feet. Nothing worse than an animal that gave up.

He was fully aware that Louise kept an ear and an eye on him, and that was fine until people understood who he was, what he was. Their uncertainty was expected at first. He'd be the same regardless. But he instinctively knew exactly who Louise was right from the moment he'd seen her handle the dog. She was one of those rare individuals where the animals came first. He was similar.

"I think she's sleeping now," Louise said.

With a start, he realized she was checking on the shepherd's vitals.

"She's doing very well, but we need to give her a couple days to just heal."

He nodded and stood. Louise locked the cage. With one last look at the dog, his voice slightly thicker than he liked, he said, "Thank you."

She nodded. "I've yet to find an animal that doesn't break my heart when they're in here."

"I don't think I could do your work," he said.

"It's hard for me too at times, but it's been my calling since forever. Like you but in a different way."

"I had years in the military K9 Unit," he said, his voice catching. "But I lost my K9 partner in a bad accident. I've been recovering ever since."

"Maybe it's time for a new K9 partner," she said with a nod to the sleeping shepherd. "And maybe a new line of employment."

He cracked a smile. "Yeah, that's partly the reason I'm here. I'm not sure what I want to do."

"Law enforcement can always use dog handlers."

"Don't think I could do straight police work."

"Well, I know Levi doesn't have a dog handler. Set up your own company, contract out to him. And, of course, there's always the military."

He gave her a thoughtful look. "Not sure what would be involved in setting up a company like that. Although, if I do go in that direction, Badger, from the group that sent me here, could possibly use my services too."

"That might be your first step," she said with a bright smile, ushering them forward, "to investigate what would be required."

"I also have to train dogs to have employable skills," he said with a quirk of his lips. "Not to mention a lot of K9 work would end up being voluntary. Like emergency search-and-rescue work. Not all counties or families can afford to pay."

"I guess it depends if you need the money or not," she said with a sideways look at him. "Besides, once your company is up and running, you could decide what constituted volunteer work. Maybe a portion of your business will end up being volunteer-based."

"True. I don't how I could make this work at the moment." He shrugged.

She smiled. "Then let me give you the name and number of somebody in town here who has a lot of connections."

"Who's that?"

"I was thinking of Flynn's best friend, Logan."

"Gunner's son," Ethan said with a nod. "He's on my list of people to contact anyway."

She stopped in the act of writing down Logan's name on a notepad. "You know Gunner?"

He nodded. "I know Gunner. I'm on my way to visit

him this morning."

She straightened. "Obviously you have plenty of connections on your own. In that case, say hi to him for me."

"I will. Take good care of the dog for me."

"Absolutely," she said. "When you come back, you better have a name for her. Once you've named her, she's yours because you won't be able to let her go."

He turned and walked out of the clinic. It was still early, but the front doors were now open, and a couple vehicles were pulling into the parking lot. Perfect time for him to leave.

He hopped into his truck, turned on the engine and backed out. Time to talk to Gunner. As he turned the truck around and headed toward the exit, his phone buzzed. He pulled off to the side and read the message. **If you're around, stop by**, Levi texted. **I heard from Stone and Badger that you were in town.**

Ethan thought about it for a moment, then dialed the phone. When Levi answered, he said, "It's Ethan. I'm meeting Gunner in an hour."

"Good," Levi said. "Stop by this afternoon then."

"Not sure when that'll be," Ethan said cautiously.

"Doesn't matter when it is," Levi said. "The door's always open." He hung up.

With a smile, Ethan tossed the phone on the seat beside him and turned onto the highway. It was nice to know Levi was here.

Now to meet with Gunner. That old soldier had fingers in many pots. What was the chance he knew something about that property Cinn mentioned? And would he know anything about K9:01?

CHAPTER 4

BY THE END of the day, Cinn sat back, groaning. She'd been sitting at the edge of her seat. As she shifted in her desk chair so her lower back got support, she could feel the relief running through her spine. She checked the clock. "How did it get to be after five o'clock already?"

She shook her head when the dogs started barking. They raced to the front door, and, as she walked toward them, wondering who was out there, they both sat down and started to whine, their tails wagging like crazy. "What's gotten into you two?" she asked in amazement. She peered out the living room window.

Of course. It was Ethan. Excited and nervous, she opened the front door. "Well, this is a surprise."

He held up a bag that smelled absolutely delicious. "And maybe this is too," he said. "But I thought I'd return the favor of friendship."

She grinned. "Chinese food is a great way to return the favor, but you didn't have to do this."

"Can't I be nice?"

"Sure." She stepped back to let him in. Inside, he handed her the bag, then crouched to say hi to the dogs. As for the dog's reactions, it was as if they'd missed seeing him for weeks. In a way she felt the same. He was a curious man. One with secrets. *A loner* maybe was a better description.

Shaking her head at her dogs' antics, she walked into the kitchen. "You can sit there and play with the dogs if you want, but I'm eating."

Soon the three followed her to the kitchen. The dogs sniffed the air, weaving around her legs.

She shooed them back toward Ethan, so she could set down the containers and grab some plates. "How did you know I liked Chinese food?"

"I didn't know," he answered. "I just hoped you did."

"Well, I love it, so great choice. How was your day?" she asked as she opened each of the six containers. "I usually just order a combo," she said with a happy sigh. "This is a luxury."

"I didn't know what you would want to eat," he said sensibly. "Where are your forks?"

"Forks and chopsticks are over there." She pointed to the drawer beside the sink.

He returned with chopsticks.

She smiled and dished up a plate for herself. The dogs were on their best behavior and lay down just a few feet away. As she was about to take her first bite, she stopped and said, "Thank you. I can't remember the last time somebody did something so thoughtful."

"Should happen more often," he said. "I love to cook, but I haven't had an inclination lately." On that note he popped a bite of food into his mouth, handling the chopsticks like a master.

His comment brought up a thousand questions. "No inclination?"

He shrugged but didn't answer.

She figured that was as far as she would get in that line of questioning. "So what did you do all day?"

Another shrug.

Not sure how to break through that wall of silence, she sat quietly and ate for a few moments. "I called the clinic to see how the shepherd was doing," she confessed. "Louise said she'll probably have to stay there for a few days, but she will make a full recovery. You did a good thing bringing her in."

He nodded. But he still didn't say anything.

Together they ate in silence. The food was fabulous, so she didn't really mind the lack of conversation. As she served herself seconds, she asked, "You want more?"

He nodded. "I'm just waiting for you to get yours."

"What, and then you'll finish it?"

He shrugged again.

"Really, you can't, surely."

Ethan opened container after container and dumped the remainder on his plate.

She laughed. "So you must still be healing from your injuries if you can eat this much," she said good-naturedly. "Although you look very capable. And I'm sure you wouldn't be on this mission if you weren't in good shape."

"The accident was two years ago," he said. He cleared his throat and then, as if rusty at sharing, added, "I spent the last six months working with Badger's group. Helping out wherever needed, building Geir's house and working at security. Basically any job they had for me I took." He gave her a lopsided grin. "It helped me reassimilate into the real world."

"Hey, understood. I can't imagine." And she couldn't. It didn't bear thinking about. She was grateful for Badger's group, whoever they were. She'd have to ask Flynn sometime if he knew them. These men all seemed to have some kind of network. As she thought about such a concept, she realized, if they did, they were the lucky ones. To have a brotherhood of men? … Priceless.

"If you can't take the shepherd after Louise gives the go ahead for her to be released, Anna could probably take her until she's adopted out." She didn't know why she persisted, but she wanted to know the dog would be well taken care of.

He still didn't say a word.

"Unless you'll stick around this area," she added slowly. Just what were his plans?

"I won't be too far away," he said. "I'll be staying with a friend in Houston."

Apparently she had to be satisfied with that. "Not very talkative, are you?"

He didn't even bother shrugging.

She sighed. "A little conversation would be nice."

He looked up at her and smiled. "A little conversation is what you're getting."

She groaned and rolled her eyes. "Okay, a little *more* conversation."

He stared at her for a moment and then asked, "What do you do for a living?"

"I'm a project manager. I work for a company that does supercomputing for companies across the state. And, on the volunteer side, I arrange for the rescues of animals from other parts of the world."

He frowned. "Other parts of the world, not those that need help at home?"

"Both," she said. "But, with global conflicts, the animals suffer along with the people. Everybody is out helping the people. They forget about the animals needing assistance too."

At that, he looked interested. "Tell me more."

She launched into a tale of how they'd been bringing animals in from all over the globe and how she farmed them out to other areas of the world. "Canada takes a lot of them," she admitted. "A lot of centers here do the same."

"And yet, so many centers are here that have animal-overpopulation problems."

"Exactly, but I'm not fussy. An animal in need is an animal that I want to try and help."

A warm light came into the depth of his eyes, and he gave her a gentle smile. "I agree. I'm surprised you don't have dozens of your own here."

She chuckled. "I have to really watch myself. I'd have every one of them here if I could. I have the two dogs. I used to have two others, but a friend of mine really wanted them, so I ended up giving those two to her. Every time I go to Anna's place, I'm always afraid I'm coming home with one more."

He nodded.

"Do you have any pets?"

He shook his head. "No. I don't. Not now. Not since I left the military." He paused, then added, "I lost my K9 partner at the time. It's been hard to open myself up to that loss again."

"I'm sorry," she said quietly. "It's hard to lose a pet anytime but, when it's a working partner as well …" her voice trailed off.

They continued to eat in companionable silence, until he said, "Today I drove past the place you were talking about."

She froze, her chopsticks in midair, a piece of broccoli perched precariously on top. She swallowed hard. "Why would you do that?"

"I wanted to see if the shepherd could have come that far."

"And could she?"

He nodded. "Quite possibly. I did track her back that far. But I want to take another look. Maybe I'll go after dinner." He glanced outside. "I've still got a couple hours of daylight today."

"But you can't track twenty miles that fast," she scoffed.

"I don't have to. I know where the possible source is, so I need to pick up the blood trail and make sure it's heading the right way," he said neutrally. "I can cover a lot of ground in a short time."

"Sure, but it's easy to lose the blood trail."

He shrugged.

"You're pretty damn sure she came from there anyway, aren't you?"

He nodded.

"What will you do?"

He didn't say anything.

She groaned. "Please don't do anything dangerous."

He moved his empty plate toward the center of the table and gave her a fat smile. "I won't. The shepherd needs somebody to look after her."

"THANKS FOR THE company," he said smoothly, "At least you won't have any dishes to do." He quickly packed up the empty containers, putting them into the bag he'd brought inside and carried it out the front door with him.

"Are you leaving already?"

He could hear the worry in her voice. Worried he would

go and do something stupid. Well, he'd done a lot of stupid things in his life. Finding the asshole who did that to the shepherd wasn't one of them.

He walked to his truck, hopped in and started the engine. It had been a long day. The meeting with Gunner had gone well. Not only had Gunner wanted to hire Ethan to provide fully trained dogs for his place but Gunner had been full of ideas as to how to help with the injured shepherd and the one Ethan was sent to find. Hearing about the possible questionable property, Gunner had become full of fire and brimstone about bringing down that place. "I know that place," he'd said. "You get the intel for me, and I'll make sure something happens."

Ethan drove away from Cinn's place, checking in the rearview mirror. Sure enough, there she was, standing on the front doorstep, leaning against the doorjamb, her arms crossed over her chest, watching him leave. A strange start to a relationship so far. But, then again, he'd been the one who had come to her house twice and had left soon afterward. She probably didn't know what to make of him.

Well, he didn't know what to make of himself either. He'd been telling himself not to go to her place, even as he bought the Chinese food, knowing he had no business there.

What was he supposed to do with that? He didn't want to be interested. He didn't want to care about anyone. He didn't want to care about anything. He'd already blown that with the shepherd. And he needed to come up with a name for her. But he sure as hell didn't know what.

And now he started to care about Cinn.

There was something about her. He loved the rescue work she did. He loved that she'd cared enough to call the vet's clinic to see about the shepherd. The attraction was there. And, because it existed, he had to deal with it—but how? He hadn't planned to get involved, but it was already too late. Apparently he had chosen the dog already. From the moment anyone suggested he give her up and let somebody else take care of her, everything inside him had revolted. She belonged with him. Now he just had to find out how.

Gunner had offered Ethan a home at reduced rent in this little town. Said it would give him a place temporarily, and, maybe if he had a home, he'd stay in the area. Gunner wanted Ethan close by to train dogs.

He drove past the rental place, checked out the property, realized it would do just fine, pulled off to the side of the road and sent Gunner a text, saying he'd take it for a week or two. At least until he figured out what he was doing. The response came back almost immediately. **It's yours free for the first month. Then we'll talk.**

Ethan smiled at that. It was so very Gunner. Then Ethan turned the vehicle back onto the highway and hit the gas.

As he drove, he considered his odd relationship with Cinn. He wasn't sure how much to tell her. This last year he'd lived more or less alone as he had healed and rejoined life. Only through Badger and the rest of the gang had Ethan slowly felt like he was back to normal.

Maybe not normal in the fullest sense but enough that being around people was more comfortable. But not so much in a relationship … That was a new step to take.

Putting Cinn firmly out of his mind, Ethan refocused on the shepherd. He'd tracked her several miles from across the road where he found her. Once he had picked up the blood trail, it had been pretty easy to see the direction she'd come from. He used GPS and Google Maps to see what was on the other side of that long stretch of land, and what it was, was that same property Cinn was talking about. It was pretty easy to put two and two together.

But he needed proof. And, for that, Ethan needed to check out the place after dark. To think somebody was using that shepherd and other dogs as expendable tools just burned him.

He wasn't somebody to judge. Not yet. Instead he was on a fact-finding mission. And, if he found out this was the place that had hurt that dog, well, … he'd come back, and he'd be on a revenge mission. He knew revenge wasn't always right, but nobody got away with hurting a dog like that. And, if they had more dogs they were hurting, Ethan would release them too. And then he would shut down that place.

If they'd done something to K9:01 …

He stopped on the high ridge, two miles away from the property. With the truck parked behind the rise, away from plain sight, he hopped out, grabbed his cell phone and water jug, and headed toward the property.

Moving steadily, he stopped when the electric fence came into view. He crouched and studied the area. Twenty acres, Cinn had said. He did a slow perimeter search first. By the time he made it back to where he'd started, he'd seen that, although the fence was electric, still men with rifles were inside, dogs at their feet. But those dogs were healthy. Although lean, they looked to be fighting fit.

So, had the female he'd rescued not made the grade? Was she one that had failed to do her job, being distracted by something not allowed? Because that bullet said they wanted her dead and disposed of, not necessarily in that order. She hadn't even deserved the mercy of a clean kill shot. Ethan studied the sentries, who were more concerned about talking with each other and smoking cigarettes than walking the perimeter.

The main house was set about an acre in. A double gate led to and from the main residence. There were other outbuildings, but he didn't see much else on the twenty acres but drought-dried land. From the power grid and the solar panels, he figured something was going on underground. It didn't have to be very deep underground, just enough to stay hidden. He crept along the front to the main gate, studying the electric fence system there.

It would be a little harder to get through the fence than he had originally thought. He walked around until he found a section where it looked like critters had dug along the fence line. From the fur caught in the wire, this was likely where the shepherd had made her way out.

He tossed a rock against the fence and saw sparks fly. Moving quietly, he carefully scoped out the spot where the shepherd had dug out a little bit deeper, a little bit wider. Then, on his back, he scooted under the charged wires, and, just like that, he was in. He shook his head. If the guards were any good, this should have been found immediately. The dog had been shot from a distance, a shot that hit her shoulder only.

Which meant they hadn't even bothered to go outside the fence to find her, nor had they bothered to find out where she'd gone. Happy to have her all alone in the wastelands. He moved to the tree line and studied the outbuildings. The two sentries were off in a different section, and this area appeared to be deserted. He walked carefully, checking into the windows one by one on the rear of this particular building. He couldn't see anything in the half-light, and he didn't dare turn on a flashlight as he heard noises and dropped down.

A door opened—probably at the front of this building—and eventually he saw several women came out; more came behind them. They looked exhausted from a hard day's work.

Two gunmen waited for them. But they seemed to be protecting the women, not holding them prisoner. The women moved slowly forward, around another corner. He crept to the corner and peered after the women to see two vans. The women were loaded up, and the first van drove off. A gunman locked the door, walking back toward the second van. He hopped in and followed the first van down the long track to the main road. They stopped at the gates and locked them behind them.

He crouched down and headed back toward the building they'd just exited. Ethan didn't see any dogs, but the property was huge, so they could be anywhere. Including out in the miles of deserted terrain surrounding the property.

As soon as the others were out of sight, he picked the lock and crept inside the building. The upper building was empty, but the stairs descended on the right side at the back. He went downstairs and found a large drug lab, a working one it seemed. He took photos and crept back outside, locking up the building after him. Now he had proof, but he also didn't dare get caught.

He sent the photos to Gunner and made his way to the next outbuilding. Nobody was there, and it wasn't locked. He went inside, did a quick sweep of the room, didn't see anything important.

Just as he was about to exit, he heard voices.

"We need a couple new gunmen for this next shipment."

"Why?"

"We'll be moving a double load this time. We have a new network, and it needs to be secret. But, because we'll be moving so much product, they want a couple more guys on it."

The other man said, "We can grab some of the men we've used before."

"They have to be expendable," said the first man said, his breath catching in the back of his throat.

"Damn. We use them off and on because they're good."

"Yeah, we need a couple who aren't so good. Or else we sacrifice these."

"Do they *have* to be terminated afterward?"

"Yes. The boss doesn't want any loose ends."

"Sure, but it's probably not a one-off, so somebody will have to know."

"Maybe, but you know what this business is like."

The second man sighed. "Well, the two brothers are around."

Silence followed for a moment. "Good. They're screwups anyway. Maybe, if they do a good job this time, he'll decide not to kill them."

"Nah, he'll kill them. I don't understand that. It's like he wants to bloody the first trail every time."

"And maybe it's a ritual for good luck. I don't know, but no way I'll argue."

The two men separated, but one of the footsteps walked toward him. Ethan crouched low in the far corner behind the door, just in case the man came inside. Ethan had taped the conversation the best he could with his phone, but he couldn't guarantee the quality.

The door opened, and a flashlight shone inside. Yet the flashlight did only a quick pass. Then, with nothing to see, the door slammed shut, and a lock popped on the outside. The footsteps slowly moved away.

Under his breath Ethan whispered, "Shit, shit, shit."

The door hadn't been locked when he'd entered, so he hadn't considered that end to his escape later. He could bust down these walls, but he didn't want to let anybody know he'd been here.

He did a quick search and, at the back, found a panel of the wall was already half warped. He applied gentle pressure and ripped loose the bottom of the boards. Dropping to his belly, he managed to squeeze through, scraping his back in the process. He couldn't stick around any longer.

His back burned, and he dared not leave blood behind. With a hand holding his shirt tight around his waist, he stayed close to the trees, following the tree line back to where he'd gained entrance under the electric fence. This time he went down on his belly to avoid leaving blood on the ground, being extra careful not to touch the wires either. As soon as he was on the other side, he stood again and shoved a bunch of rocks in the hole under the fence. It would be easy enough to find next time. But, just in case, he took a GPS reading, tracking the exact spot where he'd entered, and then he ran away from the property. He could hear voices behind him, but there wasn't anything for them to see now.

And nobody shouted. No lights were turned on. So Ethan figured, if there was some security alert, it had nothing to do with him.

Back in his vehicle, he put the transmission in neutral and let his truck roll back down the hill, the way he'd come. He was miles down the highway before he turned on the engine and lights. He pulled to the shoulder, stopping so he could call Gunner.

"Did you get the pictures I sent?"

He was spitting mad. "Yeah, I did," Gunner said. "I've already talked to a couple cops. They'll set up a raid on the property."

"Good. I managed to get in through a spot in the fence. Looks like the shepherd dug a low-lying spot under the fence. It's a little hard to get in and out, but I made it."

"Are you sure nobody saw you?"

"I'm sure. My back is bleeding, but I don't think I left any blood behind. Yet there's always that possibility. I'll get that bandaged."

"Get yourself fixed up. The police are on this. I'll light a fire under them to make sure it happens fast."

"They're moving product. I've got audio of it. I hope it's audible. Let me send it to you."

He clicked off from Gunner and listened to the information he'd recorded, then forwarded the audio file to Gunner and called him back.

"I sent you the audio file. Make sure you listen to it. Not a ton of detailed information is there, but it will help explain what's going on."

He ended the call and sat here. His back still burned. He could feel wetness along his spine as sharp pains dug at him. He was afraid he'd gotten a good splinter in there under his skin. If it had been anywhere else but his back, he could take care of it himself. Given where it was, chances were he would need help.

With that thought uppermost in his mind, he picked up his phone and called Cinn.

When she answered, her voice was slightly distracted, as if she'd been doing something. He asked, "Am I disturbing you?"

Her voice turned brisk when she heard his. "No, I was almost asleep. What's up?"

He hesitated, then said, "I don't want to disturb you. I'll talk to you in the morning." He ended the call.

Almost immediately his phone rang. It was her.

"Don't do that," she snapped. "You had a reason for calling me. Now what is it?"

He hesitated again, then said, "How are you with first aid?"

She gasped. "Are you hurt?"

"Not badly but I think there are splinters are in my back."

"Then get your ass over here." And she hung up.

He grinned. He really loved that temper. It was very refreshing and honest. And he had had very little honesty in his life. With that thought in mind, he turned on the truck and headed toward her place.

CHAPTER 5

C INN GOT UP and dressed. She had just gotten into bed and was relaxing when Ethan called, but sleep was the last thing on her mind now. Downstairs she went to the first aid cabinet. She kept a fairly extensive one because of the animals. Taking out her field kit to the kitchen table, where the light was the brightest, she located tweezers, antiseptic and sterile gauze. She didn't know how far away he was; she should have asked him. But, if she called him now, he'd be driving. She didn't want him to talk and drive, particularly not if he was already injured.

She put on coffee, sat at the table and waited. She had one cup half gone when she saw the lights coming up her driveway. She poured him a cup and brought out a bottle of whiskey she kept in the back of the pantry. She opened the door, relieved to see him walking mostly normally. As he approached, she could see the pain on his face.

She ushered him in, closed the door behind him, turned and cried out at the blood on his back.

"How bad is it?" he asked.

"I won't know until I get that shirt off you. That's a lot of blood though."

"Damn. I was trying to avoid leaving a blood trail."

"How did you even drive like that?" she asked, walking around him.

He spotted the whiskey, and his face lit up. Then he looked at the coffee.

As his gaze bounced between the two liquids, she shrugged. "If you drink some of the coffee, you can always top it up with whiskey."

He grabbed the chair, flipped it around and sat backward, undoing his shirt buttons as soon as he was seated. Ever-so-gently he extricated his arms from the sleeves. Some of the blood had dried, making his shirt stick to his back.

"Before you pull that off, let me soak it. We don't need any more damage done."

She walked to the bathroom, grabbed several washcloths, soaked them under the faucet, then returned to the kitchen and laid them across his shirt, soaking the dried blood, so it would release the shirt. It took several attempts; finally the wet shirt pulled away. She placed it in the sink and ran cold water on it, went back to the kitchen table and gently cleaned his back with a wet sponge.

Finally she saw the splinters of wood in his back. "What did you do? How did you manage to get these splinters?"

"I got locked into a building," he explained drily. "At the back wall were a couple busted boards, so, rather than making a big exit—telling them I had been there—I tried to sneak out and got caught on some of the jagged edges."

"I'll say. You'll need some of that whiskey," she warned.

Obediently he took a big slug of his coffee, reached for the bottle of whiskey and filled his cup. She grabbed the tweezers and went to work.

"I'll start with the little ones. I'm placing the slivers on a paper towel."

She set the paper towel on the table beside him. Carefully she pulled at the wood splinters until she had the easier ones out. But two were big ones, one of which was jagged. Using the tweezers, she gently got the smaller of the two out, feeling his back muscles stiffen.

"I've got the easiest ones out," she said gently.

She grabbed the gauze, put some antiseptic on it and cleansed all the areas she had cleared of splinters. His back muscles tensed at the pain, but he never said a word.

She sat on a chair next to him. "You've got a bigger one, but it's jagged. I'll have to cut the skin to get it out."

"Then you have to cut the skin," he said, his tone neutral. He discussed this like it was nothing unusual.

She sighed. She walked over to a kitchen drawer, grabbed one of her sharp paring knives, poured some antiseptic on it and came back to him again. She studied the splinter for a long moment, seeing where it was hooked in and wouldn't pull out. She sliced the skin from that hook forward. His muscles bunched underneath her hands, but he never said a word.

Amazed, she murmured, "Always got to be the strong guy, don't you?"

"I am what I am," he said quietly.

She nodded to herself, then realized he couldn't see that. "You are indeed."

She reached for the tweezers and grabbed hold of the splinter embedded in his skin. She pulled it out, all three inches of the jagged wood, and laid it on the paper towel in front of him.

He took a look and then nodded. "No wonder that hurt."

She cleaned his wounds once more, then studied the rest of his back. "Just abrasions from here on, I think." She took a long moment to clean the area thoroughly, then, grabbing the antiseptic ointment, she carefully covered the area. "That's a pretty big area to cover with gauze."

He shook his head. "I'll be fine."

"You won't be fine if it continues to bleed," she warned.

He frowned when she held up a large sheet of gauze.

"I suggest for the night we at least cover this. I can tape it down, and then you won't get any more blood on whatever clothing or bed you're sleeping in."

He nodded.

"And then tomorrow morning," she said, "you can come back, and I'll change it."

"Thank you," he said quietly.

"While you were out there playing cops and robbers, did you find anything?"

He grabbed his phone, flicked through it and held up a photo for her to see.

She peered over his shoulder and gasped. "Is that a drug lab?"

He explained what he'd seen, about the women, and when he went into the building itself.

"That was dangerous," she scolded. "Cops are around for that reason, you know?"

He chuckled. "The work I used to do was way the hell more dangerous than this," he assured her.

"That doesn't make me feel better," she snapped.

She sprayed his scrapes with an antibiotic spray, for extra prevention, then placed the gauze on top and taped down the corners. She'd have to tape the edges too. Otherwise, every time he turned while he slept, it would tug and pull.

As soon as she was done, she said, "That'll hold for the night." She motioned at the photos. "What will you do about it?"

"I've already contacted Gunner," he said. "He's contacted the police. I believe they're pulling something together now."

She sat down hard in the chair across from him. "Oh, thank God."

He looked up at her in surprise.

"I was afraid you'd go in after them yourself."

The corners of his eyes crinkled up with laughter. "If I wasn't alone, I might," he admitted. "But I don't know how many men are out there. I heard at least four."

"And all armed?"

"All armed and dangerous, and two, possibly more, highly trained dogs."

"Shepherds?"

He nodded. "But these were in better shape."

She looked at him for a long moment. "Do you think she was fired from her job?"

He shrugged. "If she was fired, it was a long time ago because she's pretty skinny."

"Or she could have been sick. No way to know."

"Not yet," he said. "We should get to the bottom of it soon enough."

She nodded. "Do you want to stay here for the night?"

His face showed his surprise.

It mirrored the surprise in her heart. She shrugged. "I meant on the couch," she said drily.

He shook his head. "Thanks, but no thanks. I have a bed for the night." He stood. In a smooth move, he straightened as if it was no big deal.

She groaned as she watched him. "You don't always have to be a big tough guy, you know?"

He smiled and repeated, "I am what I am."

"We are all what we are. But we can change."

He leaned down, and, in a surprise move, kissed her gently on the forehead. "Thanks for the first aid, Doc." And he walked back out into the night.

She looked around her kitchen. The bloody shirt was still in the sink. She wished she'd had some painkillers for him, but, by the time she thought of it, he was already in the truck and backing out. She swore softly and cleaned up. She'd been wishing for something exciting to happen, but she hadn't really expected anything like this.

"Just goes to show you that you should watch what you wish for."

THE NEXT MORNING when he woke up, it was hard to move. His back was stiff and sore. He half stumbled, half hopped toward the shower and let the hot water run down his back. Only belatedly did he remember a bandage was all across his back. He reached around and tugged at the corners. The water had loosened the tape, and the gauze was, of course, soaked to his skin, but it had, in effect, loosened from the scabbing on his back. With one corner free, he loosened the other, and then it dropped down, the water hitting his sore flesh.

He stood like that for a long moment, rotating his shoulders and neck, easing the pain. He checked the time as soon as he got out. It was almost 8:00 a.m. Normally he didn't sleep that long. But he'd taken painkillers before bed, and that seemed to have knocked him out.

As he walked to the bed, a towel wrapped around his waist, his phone rang. "Gunner, what's up?"

"They'll go in today," Gunner answered.

"I want to be with them," Ethan said.

"No. You can't. They were very specific about that. But I did try."

He swore softly. "I don't want them shooting those dogs," he said.

"I know you're trying to save every animal on the planet, but those are trained attack dogs."

"We don't know that," Ethan said with irritation. "They're trained, yes, but that doesn't mean they will attack. They aren't responsible for their training. I'm pretty sure I could get them to follow my commands. I'm after one in particular. You know that, but I'd save them all if I could."

Gunner hesitated.

"Call whoever back and tell him that I can pull the dogs off of his men. No need to kill those animals. I'm all for him taking out the bad guys, but let's not hurt any more animals."

"I know K9s have been your life," Gunner said, "but I'm not sure we can do anything to help these."

"If the police are going in without somebody to work with the dogs, the dogs will attack because they won't have any choice," Ethan said forcefully. "They'll be ordered to attack. Somebody has to be there to counter those orders."

"But those dogs don't know you," Gunner said. "Why would they listen to you?"

Ethan shrugged, then winced at the movement in his back. "I can only tell you that they will."

"I doubt the police will listen to that. They're probably more than happy to shoot the dogs."

"Sure, but the dogs have been well trained. Most likely we can use them. I don't know what their skills will be, and it'll take some time to sort it out, but you and I both know how valuable well-trained dogs are. You're looking for a couple yourself."

He could almost see Gunner nodding and thinking about it.

"At least call them," Ethan said. "It's what I do. You know that." At least it was what he did—before his accident set his life on a difference course.

"I'll call you back." Gunner hung up.

Taking the opportunity, Ethan called Louise at the clinic. "How is she?"

"Doing remarkably well," Louise said cheerfully. "It's amazing what food and water and some medical care can do for an animal. She's bouncing back nicely."

"When will she be ready to be picked up?"

"I'm not sure. I think you need to see her again and note her reaction to you, when she's not so drugged."

He thought about it and said, "Maybe this morning. I'm waiting on a phone call that could change my schedule."

"Come when you can," she said. "I've got to go. I'm heading into surgery."

He heard the *click* in his ear that said she had ended the call.

He was getting dressed, when his phone rang again. He answered it, surprised to see Cinn on the caller ID.

"Do you need me to put a clean dressing on your back?" she asked without preamble.

He froze, reached around to his back to check, and his fingers came away wet with blood. "Yes."

"Then I'll see you here in twenty then." She ended the call.

He frowned but appreciated her no-nonsense attitude.

He dressed his bottom half and left off his shirt. He would need something to protect his truck seat and something to wear temporarily. He'd already left his bloody shirt with her at her place.

With a towel for the back of the seat, wearing a disposable white T-shirt and bringing another to don afterward, he packed a bag for the day, including water and some granola bars, and walked out to his truck.

His house was about fifteen minutes away from Cinn's house, and he'd just pulled into her driveway when Gunner called him back.

"They could be leaving in a couple hours," he said cautiously. "No guarantees, but, if you're on the spot, and if you follow orders, they might let you get to the dogs first."

"Where do I meet them?"

Gunner gave him the GPS location where the meeting was taking place and a time frame.

Ethan checked his watch. "I'll be there." Disconnecting from Gunner's call, he hopped out of the truck and walked in to find Cinn taking several pancakes off the griddle, placing them on two plates.

She set them on the table, next to butter and maple syrup, and said, "You might as well eat while you're here."

He frowned at her.

She frowned right back. "Sit down."

He sat, pulling off his bloodied T-shirt. He sniffed appreciatively. "Thank you."

"You're welcome," she said, and that was the end of their conversation. She quickly dropped his T-shirt in the sink and ran cold water on it, then redressed his back.

He grinned.

She looked at him suspiciously, as she sat down to eat.

"What are you smiling about?"

"You," he said. "Who'd have thought anybody out there was as short on talking as I am."

She shrugged. "There's a time for talking, and there's a time for eating." She motioned with her fork at the stack of pancakes in front of him. "Eat."

He dug in and moaned in delight. "These are wonderful," he said enthusiastically and polished off the stack. When it was all gone, she got up, reached into the oven and pulled out a plate with more, then put it down in front of him. When he looked at her empty plate, she shook her head.

"I'm full."

He didn't need a second urging. He moved the stack onto his plate, mopping up the spare syrup, and, at a much slower pace, ate the second stack. When he was done, he pushed both plates away and said, "That was excellent. Thank you."

She carried the dishes to the sink, where she put them in hot soapy water, then poured two cups of coffee.

He was stunned to think she had gone to that much effort for him. As much as he had loved the pancakes, the fresh coffee was just as nice. He looked at his cell phone and said, "I'm heading to the clinic to see the shepherd."

She sat across from him and smiled. "Say hi to her for me."

He nodded.

"Have you got a name yet?"

He shook his head. "Hard to come up with a name. I don't really know who she is yet." He could see the understanding in her gaze; at the same time he knew just what a strange thing it was he'd just said. Most people picked a name because they liked the name. They didn't match it to the animal. He motioned at her medical supplies and asked, "Can I replace what you've used?"

"I'm not worried about it," she answered. "But, if you'll be hanging around, and you'll be doing this a lot, you might want to pick up some more bandages and gauze," she said, tapping a box of Band-Aids. "Those too."

He nodded. "Next time I'll hit a drugstore." He finished his coffee, stood, walked to the sink and, before she could stop him, he washed the dishes. He stacked them on the rack, grabbed his cell phone and keys, and said, "Thank you." And he left.

He stood out on the veranda on the top step, knowing he should say something else but not sure what. He heard footsteps across the floor, and she came to stand in the doorway behind him.

"Will I see you again?" she asked.

He turned to look at her. "Do you want to?"

Her lips quirked. "Yes."

He could feel that sense of satisfaction roiling through his stomach. "Then, yes." He smiled and walked over to his truck. She was still watching him as he turned onto the highway. He wasn't sure what was going on, but it was nice to find somebody who didn't ask too many questions.

He'd been a loner for a long time, and it felt right. But he'd known he needed to get back to civilization, around people. His social skills were still rusty, his sense of humor still off. Interaction with anyone other than at work didn't come easy anymore. That was why he always related better to the animals. He preferred them over people any day.

When he drove into the vet clinic parking lot, a couple vehicles were here already, but it wasn't too busy yet. He imagined Louise ran a pretty decent business, considering the scope of the ranching and farming in the area. He didn't know if she did large animals as well, but she probably wouldn't have a lack of business in that corner either.

As he walked into the clinic, Megan smiled. "She's really doing much better."

"Is she walking?"

Megan nodded. "With help."

He frowned at that.

She let him into the back, where the shepherd was still in the cage. "If you wait here," she said, "it's time for us to take her out. You can come with us."

The shepherd had yet to see him. He walked outside to the designated area and waited, loving the fresh air versus being inside the surgery area, with its chemical super-clean smell.

When he turned around again, the door opened, and Megan and a vet assistant walked out with a band under the shepherd's belly, supporting her.

He pointed at the shepherd, frowning. If she couldn't walk on her own, he wasn't sure he could take her with him today.

"She *is* walking. We're keeping her from putting too much weight on that hip yet."

He nodded with understanding.

The vet assistant stepped back, so Megan walked with the dog. The shepherd took several hesitant steps, then a few more. She still hadn't seen Ethan. Megan walked her to the grass, where she very carefully managed to pee.

He smiled. "She's doing so much better."

The dog, hearing his voice, turned to look at him. Something in her gaze he didn't quite understand. But she was still weak. Her tail wagged, and her ears went down, not in an offensive manner but in compliance. He crouched in front of her, giving her a chance to get used to him. She moved closer, one step at a time. When she reached him, she gave him the gentlest of licks on his cheeks. He could feel his heart melting.

He scratched her under the chin. "You'll be fine now, little one. I don't know who did this to you, but you'll be much better off now."

She nudged his hand when he stopped scratching. He chuckled and, with both hands, gave her a good head scratch. When he looked up, he saw Megan beaming, the vet assistant standing off to the side and watching the interaction.

"How has she been with everybody in the clinic?" he asked. He was pretty sure he knew the answer. The shepherd was just too damn grateful for having been taken away from that horrible life and all the pain she'd been in.

The assistant walked closer, exclaiming, "She's a sweetheart. She's never barked or snarled at any of us, even when we were hurting her, which we had to do to change her needles and her dressings," she admitted. "But she's been incredibly patient with us."

Ethan nodded. "What will we call you, girl?"

"We've all been searching for names too," Megan said. "But we haven't found anything that's perfect. If you're taking her with you, then you get to name her anyway."

"Sally," he said suddenly. "Her name is Sally."

At the name, Sally's ears perked up. She reached up and nudged his chin with her nose. He chuckled. "Sally it is then."

"It's not a very heroic name," Louise said from behind

him.

He turned to look at her. "Actually, it is."

Megan handed over the leash attached to the belt around Sally's underbelly, showing Ethan how to walk her with gentle support.

He took her around, so he could get used to helping her. When he came back to Louise, he said, "How much longer does she need assistance?"

"Animals heal incredibly quickly," she said. "The issue will be that we don't want her to overdo it. So maybe another day, two days maximum."

He smiled. "I'd be happy to take her now, if I thought she would be okay without you."

"Let's give it another day," she restated. "And how is the name Sally heroic?"

He watched Sally being led back into the interior of the clinic. At the doorway she turned and looked at him. "It's all right, Sally. I'll come back and get you tomorrow."

She gave a bark and then went inside the clinic, as if fully understanding.

He turned to look at Louise. "It's short for something."

She raised an eyebrow but waited patiently.

He smiled. "It's short for Salvation."

CHAPTER 6

C INN COULDN'T HELP it. She reached for her phone and called Louise. "Has he been there?"

"He has indeed," Louise said warmly. "He's a man of hidden depths."

"Why is that?"

"Do you know what he's named the dog?"

"No. What?"

"Sally."

Cinn sat back and thought about that. "Well, it's not a bad name," she said cautiously.

"If you know what it's short for, it's a fantastic name," Louise said. "And he did tell me."

"Oh, do share."

"He named her Sally, short for Salvation."

Cinn gave a happy sigh. "He really is a good guy, isn't he?"

"I think you'll find he's exactly the same as the rest of the men we have around here. Rory, Flynn, Stone," Louise explained. "I've talked to several of them about Ethan. They all know *about* him, but they don't *know* him. He was in the US Navy K9 Unit, had an accident, recovered, but slowly. In the meantime he lost both parents and slipped into a major depression. When he came out of that, he was lost for a while. He's part of a group, the same people who sent him here, but they are back in Santa Fe. He knows Gunner and some of Levi's men too."

"Great! They seem to know each other all across the country. Which is good because they probably need that family connection. Brothers, so to speak."

"Very true," Louise said. "Anyway, he's coming to get Sally this afternoon, providing she's good enough to go."

"Wow, that'll be interesting. Man and dog do travel, I guess," Cinn quoted badly.

"I think he's looking for a reason to stop traveling," Louise said simply. "He just doesn't know what it is and probably won't know until he finds it. Maybe not even then."

Silence filled the air for a few moments.

"Have you dropped a hint in there?" Cinn asked drily.

Laughter peeled through the phone. "Not necessarily," Louise said. "But, if something's there that you want to explore in greater detail, don't let him walk away. You don't know where he'll stop next."

"He's heading into a whole lot more trouble and probably won't be leaving except in a body bag, so don't count on Sally having a home just yet," Cinn said.

"What?" Louise asked, the confusion evident in her tone. "What is he doing?"

"He's tracked down whoever did this to Sally. And I know he's contacted Gunner to do something about it, and Gunner called the police. Ethan will make sure he stops this, and he doesn't really care if he gets hurt in the process."

"Well, maybe Sally is a good thing then. Maybe she'll encourage him to be safer, so he can look after her," Louise said. "Otherwise he could be biting off more than he can handle."

After she got off the phone, Cinn chewed on her bottom lip for a moment, wondering what she could do to help Ethan. But she didn't really have any options. She walked back into her office and stopped, looking out at the road. She saw a vehicle parked on the side of the highway. People didn't stop there, unless they were broken down. Her driveway came off the highway to her place down below, so she didn't hear or see much of the traffic—unless they parked on her side of the road. She watched and waited. Finally it turned and headed off again.

She forgot about it until a couple hours later, when she looked up, and possibly the same damn truck was parked once more on the roadside, facing the opposite direction this time. She got up with her cell phone and took a picture. It was too far away to show any details. Even if something funny was going on, who would she call? There was no reason for anybody to be watching her. The only thing different in her life right now was Ethan. And the dog.

Her breath caught in the back of her throat. She walked to a different window and peered out. It was just past noon, and she hadn't seen Ethan for hours. What if these men were looking for him? What if they'd seen him come to her house?

Unnerved, she went to call him, then stopped. Should she call him or not? She didn't know what he was doing. Not second-guessing herself, she hit the Dial button. When he answered, his voice sounded distracted.

"Any chance somebody followed you here?" she asked.

"What?" His voice was sharp. "Why would you ask that?"

"About an hour after you left, a truck parked out on the road. I thought I saw somebody looking down here at me. I didn't think anything of it because the truck started up and drove away. But, a few hours later, the same truck, or what appears to be the same truck, has parked up there again. I tried to take a picture of it, but it's pretty far away."

"Send me the picture, and I'll call you back."

She shrugged and sent him the picture with a note. **I told you it was far away.**

She went in the kitchen and put on a pot of coffee, hating the tension coiling inside. She didn't want to think he'd brought trouble to her door, but then she knew she couldn't blame him. Not only was he the kind to walk into trouble, he was the kind to deal with trouble nobody else wanted. And he had gone looking for it. He'd gone to help save Sally.

Just as the coffee was done, her phone rang.

"Stay in the house. Lock it up. I'll come back this afternoon." He disconnected.

She glared at her phone and tossed it on the kitchen counter. The last thing she wanted was to be given orders.

She looked outside and saw the truck moving away again. She smiled, grabbed her phone and sent Ethan a text. **False alarm. Truck's leaving.**

Order still stands came the instant response. **Let me know if it comes back.**

"Like hell I will," she said aloud good-naturedly.

She headed back to her office and her work. She had tons to do, and, if she was lucky, she would get something accomplished. She had another mess of emails and phone calls to make. She wanted to get through her business work and get back to her dog rescues. Just because Ethan was focused on saving Sally didn't mean other animals weren't desperately in need of her assistance.

STARING AT THE property, two cops at his side, more stationed close by, a dozen in all, Ethan hated to think somebody might have followed him to Cinn's place. He'd kept a careful eye out the night before and hadn't seen anyone. But it was possible the owners had a lookout. Once at the property, he'd been so focused on the sentries there that he'd forgotten more could be higher up.

He froze, thinking about that and then swore softly. The two cops beside him turned to look at him. "When I was here last night," he said softly, "I think a lookout might have been up on that peak." He turned to look at the hill where he'd been parked. "I parked up there and came down here. If somebody up on the top saw me …" He let his voice trail off, looking at the text on his phone.

"Why are you thinking about that now?"

"Because a truck is parked on the highway, watching a friend's house where I'd been last evening. It disappeared, then it came back. I want to make sure nobody from here followed me to her."

"Then go look after her," urged Matthew, one of the two officers.

"She says it's gone now, and she will stay inside locked up." At least he hoped she would. He motioned at the property in front of them. "I need a chance to help these dogs."

"Not if she's in danger, you don't."

He shook his head. "I don't think she's in danger. But it could mean somebody's out there looking for me."

The signal came just then. The men moved out. Ethan's military training kicked in, and he already knew where he was due to be. As he approached the front, he kept behind the policemen. His best defense was getting those dogs on his side. He just had to get to them before the place exploded in chaos.

Just then one of the armed sentries called out, "Stop. This is private property. You're trespassing."

Ethan's gaze zoomed in on the dog at his side. Her hackles were raised, and she snarled. She wore a prong collar, and it was all the guy could do to hold her back. Ethan knew, with a minimal touch, she'd go at the first intruder. Quickly using his fingers, he whistled a high-pitched tone that he'd used on his own dogs in the military—a tone that animals could hear much better than humans.

Silence followed.

The dog's barking stopped as if cut off with a knife. Her ears went up, and she turned, looking toward Ethan, her gaze intent. The handler was so focused on the men at the front gate that he didn't notice the change in the dog's behavior.

Good. Because they would need every advantage they could get.

Darkness dropped as heavy clouds moved overhead. It added a somberness to the situation. His focus was on the dogs, but he knew the other men were focused on not getting shot as they took down the operation. Not part of the inner workings of the police team, Ethan watched as they all moved into position.

On the other side of the fence, two more men arrived with two more dogs. One a big male. Was that K9:01?

The dog he had whistled to no longer pulled on her leash. She looked around, confusion in her eyes. He let out a light whistle, easing the tension in her system. She gave a headshake, as if not quite sure what was going on. Her lips curled, and she snarled again. Her handler pulled back on her leash. Ethan watched as her neck was jerked to the side with more force than necessary. Her lips curled harder, and the snarls could easily be heard from where Ethan hid.

Matthew, still beside him, asked, "Why don't we just pop a bullet in her? It'd be easier. She looks like she's ready to eat one of us."

Ethan shook his head. "Her collar has metal spikes that are digging into her neck, probably cutting her throat right now. She's been trained on torture and mishandling. It's not her fault."

"It might not be her fault," the guy said sarcastically, "but I sure as hell don't want to be at the receiving end of those teeth."

Shots fired from the left. After that, chaos ensued inside the compound. There were shouts, sirens, and the dog lunged in a frantic frenzy. Ethan knew, once the attack dogs hit that blood rage, it would be hard to control them. He had to get them away from their handlers.

One of the men lost control of his dog. It jerked hard, jumping at the fence. Instead of going after the dog, he pulled his rifle from over his shoulder and fired at the police team.

Ethan crouched below the hillock. He didn't think this was the way it was supposed to go down. For some reason he'd expected this to be a simpler operation. But, once they'd been sighted, instead of more talking, the compound had fired at them.

As quickly as it started, it stopped.

Silence hushed over his ears. He looked at the man at his side. He talked on his walkie-talkie.

Matthew bounced up, nudged Ethan and said, "All clear. One dog is injured. I don't know about the other two. We've got six shooters down and secured. You stay behind me the whole way."

Ethan did as instructed, happy to be in the background on this one. As they forced open the gates, another alarm went off, causing the dogs to howl. Ethan pulled the ropes and leads he had brought with him out of his backpack, and, with his hands well-gloved and his forearms wrapped, he headed in to the left, as all the men went to the right.

One of the dogs headed toward the policemen. The officer turned, lowered his rifle and called out at Ethan, "She's got one chance. Then I shoot."

Ethan stepped in front of the rifle. The dog jumped at him, her mouth wide, teeth shining bright. He twisted at the last moment, shoving his padded forearm in her mouth. He gravitated as her weight hit him. He went down with her, flipping her to the ground, putting his foot on her neck and grabbing control of her leash. The dog released her choke-hold on his arm and lay on the ground, quivering.

He looked at the officer, still pointing a gun at him. "She'll be fine."

The officer stared at the dog and then at Ethan with disbelief. He shook his head and said, "Better you than me. Watch out for the other two."

Ethan nodded as two more dogs approached. They were confused with their teammate on the ground. Ethan released his gentle but effective hold on her neck, waited for her to get up. With a special training collar firmly in place, he tied her to the open gate so she had no choice but to stay down. With her neck at an angle, she couldn't lunge at anybody. It was temporary until he could get the other two dogs under control.

He pulled out another lead and approached the two dogs. Two was harder than one because they would double-team him if they were well trained. He went down into a nonthreatening crouch. He whistled a high piercing sound. The dogs started to howl. And, with that, their bodies relaxed just slightly.

The dog behind him howled too. He glanced at her, but she was fine.

Instincts told Ethan to lunge and to hook on the collars so this pair couldn't turn on him. But he knew that any heavy-handed approach would bring them instantly into the red zone.

He took several steps toward the closest one. It turned its gaze on him and curled its lip, dragging its leash with each movement. All Ethan had to do was get a hold of that leash himself.

He yelled out commands, but the dogs wouldn't listen. He walked forward, his body ready for the attack he knew was coming. He needed to successfully repeat the first scenario. But this was a big male, and it didn't look like he would go down easily. Ethan braced himself, but the dog suddenly broke to the left and circled around behind him. Then it barked in front of the female, already down and tied up. Ethan couldn't keep an eye on both loose dogs, now split up.

"Very smart," he said, admiration in his tone as he backed up slightly so he could get a wider view of each one. "Are you also trying to protect her?"

He knew the officers kept an eye on what was happening. Most of them would agree that a bullet was the only answer in this situation, but Ethan didn't agree. It wasn't the animals' fault they were defending something the good guys needed to stop.

The big male, still standing in front of the captured female, barked and barked. Ethan studied him, trying to understand what his weakness was. The other male on his right lunged. Ethan deliberately kept his gaze on the second male as he went for him. Still crouched, he raised his arm to give him something to bite on. As soon as he bit, his jaw locked down, he grabbed the leash dragging behind him. With that done, Ethan put another one of his restraining collars on the second male and dropped him until he was flat on the ground. He still had a grip on him and fought. Once he released his jaws, and it would take some time, he could pull free from him. But he surprised him, unlocking his hold before he went down.

He gave him a moment, safely behind him with his hand on his throat. He talked to him in a calm, quiet voice. "Take it easy. You'll be fine."

When he stopped snarling, he gave him the command to lie down. He did.

He smiled. "I knew you were well trained."

He ordered him to stand and to heel. He stood and took his position just behind Ethan's right leg. All the while the first male, now even more confused, showed signs of attacking. Ethan was surprised he hadn't attacked at the same time as the earlier one had. Ethan wondered how much of that was due to the female behind him. Maybe the male dog felt he was the defender of all of them. Animals stayed in packs, and the first male was the alpha male obviously. Now his pack was being split and taken down, but, as long as Ethan held the leash of this second male dog, Ethan had to make sure he kept the other male contained too.

He looked around for a place to tie him up, but there was only the fence. Using commands, he moved slowly toward it. With the short leash hooked so his head, neck and chest were against the fence, he couldn't move. After securing him, he headed for the first male, wondering if this was the K9 he was looking for.

"Hey, boy. I know you don't understand this, and you're just fighting for your life. I have no intention of hurting you."

He spoke in the same tone he used to work with dogs all the time. Usually he worked with dogs delighted to be working, dogs that loved to learn, dogs that loved to have a job to do every day. But, every once in a while, he came up against animals either wild or badly abused, and those needed the same loving care he'd given his own.

This one was missing great big chunks of hair along its back and sides. Ethan didn't know if it was from mange or abuse. Scars and definitely some blood were on his shoulder. Again, who was to say where that came from? There was nothing wrong with the breadth of his jaws. The male looked like it was a good forty pounds heavier than the females, also the norm. But he also had something else about him. He wasn't a purebred shepherd from the looks of him. Ethan wasn't sure just what he was though.

He kept his gaze on the dog, knowing every action would show in the dog's eyes first. Ethan just had to be ready. He had another restraining leash in his hand and, just in case, a big choke chain. He figured the male would be the hardest to take down.

He risked a glance up and found he was surrounded by officers. "Is everything else under control?" he asked.

"Yes. By the way, this is the one that got shot."

"Hopefully it's not bad," he said. "That explains the blood on his shoulder."

"Are you sure you don't want us to give him a second

bullet?"

Ethan shook his head. "No. Just like the two others, he's only doing his job."

"And how the hell will you win this fight?" Matthew asked. "It looks like he'll go for your throat."

"He will, if I give him that chance. But there can only be one boss. And he has to understand that I mean to be that boss."

One of the men snorted.

That sound set off the big male dog in front of him. Ethan backed up several steps, giving the dog room to run, and he took advantage, seeing his prey as weaker. He lunged for Ethan's throat. As soon as that jaw opened, Ethan thrust his left arm forward into the dog's open jaws, as far as he could, forcing the dog's jaws wide, then flipped him to the ground onto his sore shoulder. The dog yelped but was already locked in place on Ethan's padded arm.

One-handed, Ethan calmly disengaged the spikes on the dog's collar he currently wore and pulled it a bit tighter so the dog wouldn't completely slip from it. Then Ethan let the dog roll over to his other side, onto his good shoulder, and stepped on the chain leash, all while the big male chomped down firmly on Ethan's padded arm. In a bold move, Ethan's free hand removed the glove from his other hand, then shoved his glove into the dog's mouth, forcing his jaws to open wider. This pushed it past the point where it could apply force to bite down, freeing Ethan's arm finally. With the dog already weakened, it couldn't do much. Nor did it try.

And, just like that, Ethan had the third one secured. While it was down, Ethan used his other leg to hold the jaw and the head firmly on the ground without hurting it and checked out the bullet wound, but it was more of a burn. Ethan studied him. His markings were close to the picture he had of Sentry, the K9:01 dog. He'd have to wait to check his tattoo to confirm his identity. The dog was already stressed; now wasn't the time to add to it.

"I don't know who shot him," he called out, "but all you did was piss him off."

The uniformed men stared at him.

Ethan looked at the three dogs and then at the policemen and asked, "What's wrong?"

They shook their heads. None were apparently concerned about more unfriendlies on the compound, so presumably the place was secure.

"Damn it. I'd rather take down six gunmen than face one of these dogs," Matthew snapped. "That was crazy."

Ethan smiled. "I used to train these guys to do just what they did. They're well trained. They did their jobs. They don't know the difference between good guys and bad guys in this case," he said. "They don't deserve a bullet for having had no choice."

"Yeah, but now what will you do with them?"

"It depends what the law will allow me to do," he said. "I have a place I can take them. I have a vet to get this one treated. I'd like to rehabilitate them, so they're good protective animals."

The officer in charge, Sergeant Mendelsson, walked toward him, his hands on his hips. The male shepherd growled.

Ethan applied gentle pressure on the dog's jaw to let him know what was acceptable and what wasn't. "If you just stand your ground there," he said to the sergeant, "the dog will understand that, A, I'm the boss, and, B, he's not in any danger."

The sergeant nodded. "I think I can arrange that. I don't know what will happen to them long-term."

"Destroyed, I would imagine," said another officer, approaching. "But, if you think you can rehabilitate them—and, after what we've seen here today, I think maybe you can—we'll do our best to give you that chance. But you need a place to move them."

Ethan nodded, his mind spinning rapidly. "I have a house at the moment. It is fenced. But I'll need a better way to train them. Still, I can arrange that."

"You got your chance then. What about your truck? You'll need a canopy or something for them."

He considered the options and shook his head. "The canopy would be better, yes, but I can secure them in the back so they're not going anywhere."

The men nodded.

Matthew said, "As much as I don't want to get close to them, do you need a hand moving them?"

Ethan shook his head. "I'll take them one at a time."

He lifted his foot and ordered the male to stand. Struggling with his bad shoulder, the male shepherd rose. Ethan commanded it to heel, and he walked the dog just like that out of the compound. He knew the men were watching, and he knew they didn't understand. And that was okay because it was what Ethan did. Only he had to stop and think about that because it was not what he did now. What he used to do was train these animals for military scenarios—to sniff out bombs, chemicals and weapons.

Potentially, in this case, he could rehabilitate these dogs to be used as guard dogs or maybe, once again, chemicals- and weapons-sniffing dogs. He had no clue where this was taking him.

What he did know was it felt right. What he did was worth it for the animals.

At his truck, he opened the tailgate and ordered the dog to jump. Instantly he jumped into the back. With the dog in the bed, Ethan secured it to one of the hooks. He couldn't take it very far like this; it wasn't safe, but he had limited options at the moment.

With one dog secured, he walked back to the fence and snagged the other two dogs waiting. With one on either side, he walked them to where the big male was. As soon as they realized where they were going, they were happy to follow. They jumped into the truck without any problem. He secured one across from the big male and then secured the third along the tailgate with it closed. None of them had enough leash that they could jump free, and, short of somebody throwing them over the side of the truck bed, no way they would get hurt.

He walked back to the sergeant and said, "Here's my address and phone number. I'll be there until I find better lodging for all the dogs, a place with kennels."

The sergeant shook his hand. "That was a nice job today. How well trained do you think they are?"

"Very well trained," he said. "I'll have to test them further to confirm, but I used to train dogs for bombs, weapons and chemicals missions. I'll run these dogs through the tests and see what they've been trained for."

The sergeant nodded and said, "I can't guarantee it, but you know what? If we can arrange it for you to keep them, and you think you can train them, we can always use dogs on specific jobs. We have almost no K9 Units here. And certainly none as well under control as you have those."

"I'll keep that in mind," Ethan said with a smile. "I've also got a female that came from this property as well. She's at the vet right now, recovering from surgery. Theoretically that's four good dogs that could be put to work."

"You might need another handler," one of the men called out.

Ethan nodded. "I might. First let me see how we do with these dogs."

With all the niceties taken care of, Ethan walked back to the truck. With a gloved hand, he reached down and gently stroked the back of the female, then the smaller male. As he approached the alpha male, he could hear the growl in the back of his throat, but he gently touched the dog on the back of his neck, letting him know Ethan was not an enemy. Then he hopped into the truck, turned on the engine and headed home.

CHAPTER 7

W HEN CINN DIDN'T hear from Ethan, and she saw no sign of him, she couldn't settle. She wandered around the house, unable to do much as she waited for news. Dark clouds had moved in overhead, and the atmosphere had an ugly feel about it. The humid static in the air made her sticky at the same time as it made her edgy. What she really wanted was for the storm to break to release all that tension. Instead, it just seemed to sit heavily above the property.

Finally her phone rang. She picked it up to hear Ethan's voice on the other end. Overwhelmed with relief, she snapped at him. "Is this really the earliest you could contact me to let me know you are okay?"

Silence hung like the heavy, dark clouds above her.

"No," he said thoughtfully. "I might have called while I was in the middle of gunfire. Or I might have called when I was facing three extremely angry dogs, who were ready to rip out my throat. Or maybe when I was explaining to the sergeant afterward that the dogs were worth saving. Or maybe when I was driving with all three shepherds tied down tight in the bed of my truck."

"Okay, so now I feel like a piece of shit," she said jokingly. "Please tell me all that happened calmly and quietly, and that none of you were hurt."

"I have a big male shepherd cross here that's got a burn

on his shoulder from a bullet. But that appears to be the only injury, which is rather remarkable considering a lot of dead bad guys are at that place."

She gasped. "Seriously?"

"They opened fire on the cops." His tone said he didn't give a damn about the dead men. "I was more concerned about saving the animals."

"So was it a drug lab?"

"As far as I know it was," he said. "Did you hear that part about I cared more about the animals? Once I had them calmed down and secured, I didn't want to leave them there for the cops to change their minds. If Animal Control becomes involved, I figured the animals would be taken to a cage and probably put down as soon as possible. I wanted a chance to rehabilitate them, to see just what they were trained to do."

"So now you have four dogs to look after?" she asked incredulously.

"Apparently four vicious dogs," he said cheerfully.

She stared out the window. "Why?"

His voice gentled as he answered, "Because I can."

She sagged into the kitchen chair and thought about that. "It won't be an easy job," she warned. "I thought you were looking for something different or some sort of new start."

"Can you really think of any better start than helping some animal with no future? Or, in this case, four?"

She sighed. "You know who you're talking to. I'm the one who moves hell on earth to get animals in desperate situations moved to new countries where they can have a chance."

"Exactly." His voice was quiet and pensive. "I saw those

dogs and the guns pointed at their heads, and I realized how much I could do to help them. They have really good useful lives ahead of them. They were doing a job. It's not their fault that job has now been taken away from them."

"Do you think you can retrain them to do what you want them to do?"

"Absolutely," he said. "That process is already in progress. Whether they like it or not, they now see me as their new leader. We'll have to do some heavy training and come to an agreement of sorts. But I'm pretty sure we're well in hand."

"But you need a place suited for these animals," she stated.

"Yes. That's a bit of an issue. I'm at the house I rented here in town where I'm staying," he said thoughtfully. "I might look for a place with kennels, or at least a big enough spot for kennels I can pull together fast for them."

"That won't be cheap," she warned. "You don't just need kennels but you also need a training space." She could almost see him nod in agreement. "This is rather sudden, isn't it?"

"Sure, but necessity is what drives a lot in our lives," he said. "I have to try."

She nodded. "I understand. The thought of having three killer dogs at your place is enough to terrify almost anybody. And a fourth to join them soon."

"What if I said they follow my commands and listen to the orders I give?"

"Seriously?"

"Yeah, absolutely. Give us a few days, and we'll have a completely different relationship."

"But how will they view the rest of the world?" she

asked. "You don't live on an island. You look after dogs ready to kill at a moment's notice. That won't sit easy with the townsfolk in general."

"No, but it's not that bad," he said. "It's not about dogs that will kill at a moment's notice because every animal has that potential. But it's knowing a dog will attack when instructed. And not just attack but attack properly. These dogs need some more training. No doubt about it. That male would go for my throat. He needs to learn to disable, not to kill."

All the horrible scenarios ran through her head, and she couldn't believe what she had heard. "This is so much above what most of us deal with."

"Which is why I have to do this," he exclaimed. "And I get it if that makes me something you don't want to be around …"

"No, that's not what I meant at all." She groaned. "I guess I'm shocked at how fast this all happened. You went up there to hopefully help these dogs, but I didn't expect you to take them away with you."

"I did," he said calmly. "There really wasn't much else in the way of options. They could have been put down on the spot, or Animal Control might have come and taken them, but the end would have probably been the same. But did Animal Control have the ability to remove these dogs safely? I doubt it. I was the best option."

"That is often how it is," she admitted. "If the dogs are a problem, they take them out."

"Exactly," he said. "So I stepped in. Now the question is whether I can make them do the job they need to do and have a decent life or whether I'll have to make a difficult decision down the road and put them down myself."

She winced. "Ouch."

"No," he said. "That would be almost impossible for me to do."

She smiled. "So when do I get to meet them?"

"Not for several days," Ethan said quietly. "As much as I would like to think they would allow strangers into their space, for the first few days, if not a week, it will need to be just them and me."

"That makes sense," she said lightly. What did she expect? It wasn't like the dogs would accept Ethan into their world easily, and they sure as hell wouldn't accept her, a complete stranger, either. "Can you add the injured shepherd to this group?"

"I think she was part of this group to begin with. I'm pretty sure she belongs with them," he said. "I have to see what kind of reaction I get when I reintroduce her. She's still weak and needs care for quite a while. If the other dogs won't accept her, I can't keep them together."

She winced. "If those dogs are vicious to Sally ..."

"I know," he said. "Which is why it needs to be just us for a while."

She nodded and smiled.

"Any sign of that truck again?"

Startled she remembered the truck she'd seen up on the highway. "I never did see it again. I'm taking a look now." She walked over to the window but saw no sign of anything. "I think I was just being supersensitive," she said. "With you going after this group, I don't know, I guess for some reason it made me nervous."

"Of course it did," he said in reassurance. "That's normal, and it's not an issue. I'm glad you at least thought to let me know it was there."

"Why?" She laughed. "It's not like you were close enough to do anything about it."

"That's true," he said. "But I could have been there within a few minutes, and I would have called somebody closer to help."

She smiled. "Well, if I see it again, I'll let you know."

"Let me know if you see *anything* odd again," he urged. "Just because the raid went off successfully doesn't mean the police got everyone."

"Thanks," she said. "I really needed to think like that."

"Yes, you do," he said as if not understanding her sarcasm. "One should always be aware."

Sure enough, as soon as she clicked off her phone, instead of feeling better about what he'd said, the reminder that the truck had been there on the highway made her feel worse.

She needed an outlet for her nervous energy, so she changed into her running gear. With the dogs barking happily at her side, she grabbed a water bottle and headed out the back door. It was late in the afternoon, almost evening, and the worst heat had started to settle back.

She opened up the back gate to the state land and took off at a fast run. With the dogs running happily at her side, she crisscrossed over the terrain, checking out some of her favorite spots, shaking off the tension of the day and her added worries about Ethan. She hadn't realized just how much she had been focused on Ethan. You had to love a man who would go in after the dogs.

But she wasn't sure his particular project would be worth his time and trouble. And that felt awful coming from her. After all, she loved animals, and she spent so much of her time trying to save animals in need. What was it about these

particular ones that scared her? Of course it was the vicious-
ness to them. But, if Ethan could tame them, or at least keep
them as well-controlled animals, then she was all for it. It
would also likely keep him close by, and that made her
happy.

She had no business looking at a relationship with
somebody who was such a loner, someone without roots,
especially when she was such a homebody. She did take trips
around the world for these animals, but so much of it
nowadays was communication on the Internet and phone. It
was easier to send photos and vet reports back and forth than
to fly over and look at the animals.

With the sun going behind the clouds, she dashed into
the trees. Racing through them, her heart felt lighter with
every step she took. Such interesting weather, a day full of
light and shadows, not hot, not cold. By the time she burst
through the other side, she was sprinting all-out. She could
feel the tension inside desperately needing the outlet. Her
feet pounded the ground as she ran faster and farther.

And then her energy seemed to wane, and she slowed her
steps, laughing, and stumbled.

Crack.

She cried out as her shoulder exploded with pain, and
she fell to the ground. She instinctively reached a hand to her
shoulder and rolled over. Panic set in, but she was a good ten
or twelve feet from the next set of trees. She pulled her hand
away, seeing the blood pumping sluggishly from the wound.

She'd been shot!

She pulled out her cell phone while she lay here, panicked somebody would come closer for a killing shot, and
dialed Ethan's phone. The dogs whimpered at her side,
unsure of what happened but knowing something had.

"I've been shot," she said baldly. "I'm about two miles from the house, on the state land behind my place. Parallel to the highway. There's a large wooded area. I've gone through that, and I'm on the field between it and the next set of woods."

"I'm on my way," he said, his voice unnaturally calm. "How bad is the wound? Did you call 9-1-1?"

"Not arterial and, no, not yet. I called you and will call Flynn next." Her voice was shaky. "It's in the shoulder."

"I'll be there in a few minutes," he repeated.

"I want to run for the trees and try to hide." She peered through the long grass. "But I'm worried about taking a second hit."

"Can you see anyone?" he asked, his voice sharp.

In the background she heard Ethan slam a door, then turn on the engine. He was already on his way. Thank God. "Where are you? How long until you get here?"

"Make that eight." His voice was even and controlled. "Put pressure on that wound. And you stay alive until I get there. Do you hear me?"

She groaned, tears pouring down her face as the pain really set in. "I'm not planning on going anywhere. But I'm a sitting duck, if somebody comes after me."

"Don't move around," he cautioned. "Just lie there and don't make a sound. There's a good chance they'll assume they caught you with the first shot."

"And the dogs? They're milling around me."

"Can you get them to lie down? That's a common behavior for a dog, or at least have them sit at your side as they wait for help to come."

She instructed both dogs to sit and lie down beside her. Whining, their noses nestling against her, they obeyed. "Is it common for dogs to stay here like this?"

"Yes. They won't leave an injured owner."

"What about a dead one?" she whispered, trying to keep her tone light as panic threatened to choke her and as her heart slammed to get out of her chest. "I keep thinking somebody's coming toward me."

"Watch the dogs for that kind of a reaction," he said quietly. "I'm already on the highway."

"Good." Her voice was still shaky, the tears easily sounding in her tone. "The dogs are sitting here, whining, but they don't act like anybody's around."

"Good. Don't run for the trees because that will let somebody know you're still alive."

"Hopefully you'll see them before I will," she joked. "If you're coming from the opposite direction as the vet's, it should only be minutes after that bad corner until you see the first copse of trees."

"Can you give me any better directions as to where you are?"

She tried explaining where the turnoff was to one of the side streets and that she was just past it. She gasped from the effort, lying quiet for a moment, then she continued, "When you get to Cotton Road Drive, I'm probably another fifty to one hundred yards past the trees right there at that turnoff."

"Coming up to the turnoff now."

"The shot came from that direction."

"Good. I'm pulling over here. You stay where you are. I'll be there in a few minutes."

She wanted to look around to search for him, but she couldn't hear any sound of a truck engine. The traffic should be audible from where she was, but she heard nothing. She held the palm of her hand flat against her wound, part of her

T-shirt balled up against it, trying to press down hard on it. She stared at the cloudy sky and focused on breathing deeply.

But surely they'd know if they caught her in the shoulder, not in the head.

This was a shitty end to a rough day. She had to think it was related to Ethan because nobody out here hated her. At least she didn't think so. She hadn't spent a lifetime creating enemies. She was one of those charity workers, and few people even knew where she lived.

She took several more deep breaths, trying to force back that panicked edge. The pain, if she thought about it, was crippling. To calm down she made a quick call to Flynn. He swore and demanded answers. "Can't talk," she said. "Just come." And she hung up.

Her ears were on overdrive for any sound, good or bad, coming toward her. But Ethan was right about one thing: watch the dogs. They were both relaxed but worried. Their noses pushed eagerly into her hand as she tried to calm them. But they weren't growling or jumping to their feet or racing toward anyone or away from anything. So, as far as she could tell, nobody was out here.

And then a dog barked. She twisted but couldn't see anything for the tall grass around her.

Soon she heard a high-pitched sound and a man's hard voice snapping orders. She couldn't confirm if that was Ethan or not. She wanted to sit up but knew she shouldn't.

Then a whistle, several barks and another whistle. And she now realized what she'd heard. *Ethan.* He'd come with one of the new dogs. She frowned. "Is that a good idea, Ethan?"

She slid to a half-sitting position, holding her shoulder,

and she could see him at the tree line, and the dog was free, tracking somebody.

She could hear shouting, as if somebody else was countering the orders.

Another shot was fired and then another. She flattened against the ground, grateful none were directed at her. But had the dog been shot? Ethan?

What the hell had Ethan done? What the hell had she gotten into?

She waited with bated breath as she tried to understand what else was going on. The dogs were no longer lying at her side but stood, studying the area, barking at the other dog, easily giving away Cinn's position. So who would find her first?

And then, in her heart and mind, she knew there was no competition. It would be Ethan all the way. And suddenly she heard footsteps coming toward her. She froze. Her dogs growled. And then a strange dog barked and raced toward her. It loomed over her, and she curled protectively into a ball, until she heard Ethan issue a command. Immediately its butt hit the ground, and its nose went out, ears up.

She let out her pent-up breath as she watched this huge shepherd stare down at her. It wasn't growling at her; it wasn't attacking her. It was as if giving a command to its owner, saying, *I found her.*

And suddenly there was Ethan.

She burst into tears. She would have thrown her arms around him, but her shoulder was killing her. He crouched at her side and stroked her face gently.

"It's all right. You're safe."

He pulled her hand off her shoulder. "Let me take a look." Then he nodded. "It could be much worse." He eased her into a sitting position and checked the back of her shoulder. "It went through, and that's good."

She shook her head. "I don't know how you can think that's good. I've been *shot*."

"Yes, you have," he said and, taking out his pocketknife, dug something out of the dirt behind her. Then he exchanged the knife for a sheet of paper from his notepad in his pocket and pulled up the slug.

She stared at it. "I really was shot?" she said in disbelief. It was one thing to assume she'd been shot; it was another thing to see the proof in his hand. She glanced around. "How do you know it's safe? Is he gone?"

"He's gone," Ethan said.

"Gone? I heard more shooting."

Ethan nodded. "He tried to countermand the dog. This, by the way, is Bella."

She looked at the shepherd, still in her position, not having been released from the command given. "Is she safe?" Cinn asked tentatively. "She's pretty ferocious looking."

"The big collar doesn't help, but it does give her name," he said. He turned to Bella and gave her a hand signal and said, "Relax."

Bella, her tail wagging, leaned over and sniffed Cinn. She reached up a tentative hand. Bella placed her nose in her hand and nudged it.

Cinn smiled and scratched Bella's head. "Did she find me?"

"Yes, she did. Not that you would have been hard to find with the other dogs here."

Both her dogs milled around Bella. The three were getting to know each other. Bella showed no signs of aggression. "How did you know she was the one you should bring?"

Cinn asked, dazed. "That was taking a hell of a chance."

"The only chance I took was if your shooter might have had better control over Bella. But I don't think she has any loyalty to the abusive men who kept her before."

"How sad is that?" Cinn murmured. "You didn't explain what the shots were I heard."

"He tried to shoot her," Ethan said quietly. "But Bella dodged and managed to miss the bullets, and, when he realized she was still coming after him, and then he saw me too, he turned the gun on himself."

"What?" Her jaw dropped. "Are you serious?"

Grim-faced, Ethan nodded. "I'm serious. We need to get the cops here now, before anybody else finds out what's happened."

He helped her stand, then led her to a large rock to sit down. He called Bella over and ordered her to guard. She stood, facing out to the world around her, her attention focused around them.

Cinn, who had a lot of experience with dogs, but none with actual working dogs of this nature, watched in amazement as Bella appeared to keep a close eye on everything going on. "What happens if I get up and walk away?"

Ethan chuckled. "Well, I guess we'll find out if you try it, won't we?"

She frowned up at him. "That's not funny."

But he was already calling somebody on his phone.

"Who are you calling?"

"The team I joined on the raid this morning."

He walked away a few steps to have his conversation. She heard bits and pieces, enough to know he was explaining the circumstances.

She reached down to pet her beautiful dogs, giving them

each a cuddle. They were not Bella by any means. They were nervous and worried and staying very close. Yet they weren't intimidated by Bella. On the contrary, they were doing their best to make friends. But Bella would have nothing to do with it. She was on guard, and the dogs were completely not there as far as she was concerned. It was fascinating to watch. And, if Cinn hadn't been in so much damn pain, she'd have appreciated it a whole lot more.

When Ethan turned to look at her, putting away his phone, she asked, "How long?"

"He figures about thirty minutes. He'll get here faster if he can. He wanted to know if you wanted an ambulance."

She shook her head. "Hell no."

"You still have to go to the hospital and get stitched up." He stood with his legs slightly apart, his hands fisted on his hips, as if ready for a fight.

She nodded. "I know. But no reason you can't drive me there." She glanced at her shoulder and said, "Hell, I can probably drive myself. It's my left shoulder."

"No, you're not driving yourself," he stated firmly. "Of course I can drive you. I told him that you wouldn't want an ambulance because you'd try to drive yourself."

She went quiet. "You don't know me well enough to be sure I'd react that way," she said but realized she was arguing futilely over nothing. The pain had kicked in heavily.

He picked up her water bottle and handed it to her. When she tried to unscrew the top, he pulled it back, unscrewed the top for her and held it out again.

She took a long drink. "That feels better," she whispered. "You don't know just how rough things are until you realize you're arguing over nothing, and it's all you can do to sit upright."

He crouched at her side and checked her over. "Did you hit your head when you went down?" he asked, his fingers gently searching her temple and the back of her head.

"No," she said, closing her eyes and leaning into the gentle massage. "But that does feel good."

His fingers deepened the pressure slightly, moving down her neck, then to her good shoulder and back. "If that's the only wound, we'll put this down to pain and shock," he said. "Not to mention you were probably running flat-out before you were struck, so you're dealing with exertion and probably a lack of water at the same time."

On that note, she drank most of the rest of her bottle, then handed it back to him. "I'm worried about the dogs too."

"Why?"

"Because I don't want to leave them alone when I go to the hospital."

"You leave them alone all the time, don't you?"

"I do, but they're pretty upset right now." She turned to look at her three-legged dog. He lay right beside Bella. She smiled. "It's almost as if he's decided Bella will protect him too."

"Animals know who and what they all are. They won't argue with Bella."

"But you haven't explained how you knew Bella was safe to bring."

"I was out back working with them, and, when I issued orders, Bella followed them instantly. She hasn't been at that place very long, and, wherever she came from, she was well trained. A couple commands she didn't know because they're very unique to the military work I did. But she's certainly been trained as a guard dog. And as an attack dog."

At the word attack, Bella slipped him a half look, and her ears went up.

He smiled and said, "No, Bella, just guard."

She relaxed but continued to stare out around the area, her head moving from side to side ever-so-slowly, as if she were keeping up a full 180-degree search. At one point, she got up and walked around several times, looking out into the trees around them.

"Is she not happy about the trees?"

"She's aware of the body over there."

At that reminder, Cinn winced. "Right."

"And death does affect the animals."

"Maybe, but in this case, he tried to kill her too."

He pointed to Bella's shoulder, where it had a bit of a burn mark. Cinn hadn't even seen it. She'd been so focused on her own pain. She gasped and leaned forward. "He almost did kill her," she exclaimed.

"Well, he tried. But he missed, and, when she got around behind him, and he saw me coming at him too, I think he realized he wouldn't have much of a hope. Before she got him, he decided to take the easy way out."

"Does that mean they've used these dogs to kill people?"

Silence was his only reply.

She turned to look up at him. "Seriously?"

His face was grim. "It's a possibility."

"That's not the dog's fault though," she said. "They can't put her down because of that."

"I don't know that we can prove that's what those guys did. But he certainly took an easy way out, and he took it fast."

"You should find out who he is," she urged. "Before the cops get here."

He looked at her in surprise.

She shrugged. "I don't know how much the police will tell us after the fact."

"Glad to know we both think alike."

Her thoughts still fuzzy, she gazed up at him in confusion. "How is that?"

"Because I already checked. His name is Gary Foster."

She frowned, rattling through her brain to see if that name meant anything, but then she shook her head. "I don't know him."

"Neither do I," he said, "but I have a photo of his driver's license and credit cards."

"Do you have anybody who can track down who he is?"

He shrugged, but, in a cheerful voice, he said, "Maybe."

She'd take that to mean a definite yes. She smiled. "This is something you know how to handle, don't you?"

"Wherever there are assholes in the world, there needs to be people who protect the innocent from them. I've always been one of the protectors." He gave her a gentle smile.

She nodded. "I figured as much. I thought at first maybe you were a new recruit for Levi's team. But now, you know something? I think you need to have your own team. A canine team."

He studied her face in surprise. "I'm beginning to think so too. And fits in with the rest of today."

"Why is that?" she asked.

In the distance she could hear sirens. She sure hoped they were for them. She didn't want to deal with the cops, but she really wanted to go to the hospital, if only to get some pain meds, to get her shoulder taken care of and then to get back home to bed, where she planned on staying for a hell of a long time.

"I told the police team I was with today at the drug-manufacturing property that's what I was looking to do."

When his words sank in, she stared at him in astonishment. "Wow. Still, if you can make Bella do what Bella's doing, I think there'd be all kinds of work for you."

"It's not as if I'll be running down killers," he said, "but, if Bella has other training, … or I can enhance her existing training—for all the dogs, not just her—then we could work for many agencies."

"I think there'll always be work for well-trained dogs."

"I guess we'll see, won't we?"

ETHAN WASN'T READY to make any plans yet. In the distance he could hear sirens and other vehicles approaching. He smiled down at her and said, "The cavalry is coming."

Instead of looking pleased, she'd winced. "I'd rather go straight home."

He studied the level of pain evident on her face. "We'll get you out of here as soon as possible."

"No ambulance though," she warned.

"I told you that I'd drive you," he said quietly. "But I may have to deal with the police first."

"So that's the trade-off," she said quietly.

He crouched in front of her. "You hang in there." He could see her pain-fogged gaze deepening. Worried, he said, "Forget it. I'll tell the cops I have to take you to the hospital first. Then I'll come back and talk to them."

She gave a strangled laugh. "It's not that bad. Besides, the cops won't let you leave the crime scene."

"Well, they won't leave you here either," he warned. "So

it's me or the ambulance."

Suddenly Bella growled, a sound that raised the hairs on the back of Cinn's neck.

"Not quite," a stranger called over.

Ethan spun, squatting low, until he saw Flynn standing a safe distance away.

Ethan glanced at Cinn.

She nodded. "I sent out a distress call to him too."

Slowly Ethan rose on his feet, standing protectively at Cinn's side. "Bella, stand down."

The dog relaxed, but her gaze never left Flynn.

Flynn nodded and approached. "The cops are here. We'll let them talk to her, and then I'll take her to the hospital."

Ethan was of two minds, but she needed to go to the hospital, and he needed to stay here with the cops. He glanced again at her, but she was smiling up at Flynn.

"Thank you. I'd love the assistance." She reached up with her good arm to Flynn. He carefully helped her to stand on her feet, staying right beside her in case she fell.

Ethan watched the color drain from her face with the movement. But he deliberately didn't take a step closer. Independence was fine, but it was also a good gauge to see a person's will to live. And, in her case, she was doing just fine. He nodded at Flynn and said, "If you don't mind ..."

Flynn gave a clipped nod. "I know Cinn well. She'll be fine with Anna and me."

Ethan realized he was not being butted out but being reassured that Cinn would be okay. And then it didn't matter how reassuring Flynn was because they were suddenly surrounded by police. Bella didn't like being crowded. She growled and moved back slightly.

Two of the men appeared to know Flynn. But nobody knew Ethan. They weren't the cops he'd worked with earlier, so they must have called a detachment closer to the scene. He stayed quiet as discussions about what happened went on. And finally the men turned to him. He stared back, his gaze flat.

One of the men frowned at him. "Where's the dog?"

He pointed twenty feet off, where Bella still lay on his command.

"How dangerous is she?"

"In the wrong hands she's a killer," he said calmly. "In the right hands she's a savior."

The officers didn't like hearing that.

Flynn spoke up, "It's like anything." His voice was quiet but authoritative. "Dogs and guns are both weapons if they are used that way. The fact of the matter is, she's been standing guard over Cinn to make sure nobody else comes after her. And that is priceless."

Ethan wasn't so sure that was the case, but he had brought Bella on purpose. He looked at the leader of the police group and said, "I was working with law enforcement out of Houston earlier today." He mentioned Sergeant Mendelsson's name. Several men nodded. "You can verify with him that I'm the real deal."

The commander motioned to one of the men. He stepped back and pulled out his phone. "I'm calling to confirm Ethan Nebberly's identity."

Ethan stood, his stance casual but alert, his arms crossed over his chest, but he would go from zero to sixty in two seconds flat if he had to. In the meantime, he glanced at Bella. Her ears were up, her shoulders hunched, and, though she was in a lie-down position, she watched every move

Ethan made. He had to remind himself that she was watching his hand signals. If he made the wrong one, there could be a disaster. He looked at the commander and said, "We can stand here and wait for confirmation, or I can show you the body, and we can go from there."

"What body?" the commander asked sharply.

Ethan motioned at Cinn. "The man who shot her."

"Did you kill him?"

Ethan shook his head. "I didn't have to. The dog went after him. He tried to countermand my orders on the dog. When she wouldn't listen to him, he turned the gun on himself."

The officers studied Ethan, as if trying to figure that out. Ethan shrugged and waited. It didn't matter to him what they said. If they were any good at their jobs, the evidence would prove his story to be true. He looked over at Cinn and said, "I'll see you at the hospital in a bit."

The men looked at her, and the commander asked, "Are you okay to go on your own? Do you need an ambulance?"

She took several steps with Flynn beside her all the way. "I'm heading there now. I'm ambulatory, so no need to waste anybody else's time."

The commander said, "I'll meet you at the hospital later then. I need your statement."

"I can tell you right now. I was hunted down, shot and stayed flat. I called for help. Both these men came to my assistance. Ethan arrived a good forty minutes ahead of Flynn. Ethan went after the shooter. Just as he said, I could see them in the trees, and then there were gunshots. Once Ethan knew I was no longer in danger, he came to me. But now I have to admit, I'm feeling pretty shitty. So if you'll excuse me ..." She gave everyone a wan smile and then grabbed Flynn's forearm.

Gently he led her away from the group.

Ethan watched them go.

When she was a good ten to twenty feet away, she turned to look back at him and whispered, "I'm fine."

Seeing that, hearing her voice, something inside him relaxed. He turned to look at the policemen and said, "Shall we? You may want to mark this spot," he added, pulling the paper-wrapped slug from his pocket, "where I found this."

One of the officer's had gone back to the police cars and arrived now with cones and markers. They staked out the spot where Cinn had been shot.

Ethan pointed where his vehicle was parked up on the other side of the tree line on the highway. "You can walk up there and confirm that's my vehicle. I headed here from that spot right into the tree line. Now I'll take you where the body is."

He stepped forward and snapped his finger, bringing Bella to his side. He reached down a hand, and she nudged his fingers with her nose. Gently he stroked her forehead. He wondered at anybody who could abuse such a beautiful, obedient, well-trained animal who was just looking for somebody to love.

The commander stepped up beside Ethan, but his gaze was on Bella. "The sergeant confirmed your identity. He also said that you subdued three dogs, even though the officers were all ready to shoot them, and that you appeared to have good control over them."

"It's what I do," he said simply. "Over eight years in the military working with dogs. I wasn't about to let them be shot just because they had shitty owners."

The commander fell silent at that. "We do the best we

can," he said, "but, if we can't get a dog to not attack us …" and he left his words hanging.

Ethan nodded. "Understood. But I was there. And Bella, as you can see, although I didn't train her, is extremely obedient."

"Don't different trainers have different commands?"

"Yes, but some commands are universal. I don't know all she can do yet," he admitted. "I'm hoping to find out more about her and the others. She is by far the most amiable. I have the other two dogs back at my place. Plus an injured one currently at the vet that was badly abused and shot."

The sergeant whistled. "Asshats."

Ethan agreed, but he had a lot harsher words for them.

It took another few minutes to walk into the trees. He reached down, caught Bella's attention and ordered her to find the man who shot himself, then unhooked her leash. Bella bounded forward. She headed farther into the trees, stopped for a moment, took a slight adjustment in her direction and went left. Ethan followed.

The commander asked, "How can you be sure she's not tracking a squirrel?"

"I can't," he said cheerfully. "But she has no love lost for that man. She went after him instinctively and with way too much eagerness."

"You think he abused her?"

"Abused her or possibly had a hand in training her. But there was no love in the training. If anything, what I saw when she went after him was hate."

"Were you capable of calling her off?"

Ethan nodded. "It was close, but, yes, she did finally come at my command. But, when the guy saw me and the dog working together, and he realized he couldn't get Bella to do what he wanted her to do, he turned the gun on himself."

"But there was no reason for him to kill himself. He could have just shot you and Bella instead."

Ethan gave a hard laugh. "I can't be killed quite so easily as that."

Soon they were upon the body. Ethan stood at the perimeter and waited while the cops approached. The gun was still in the man's hand, but there was no way to mistake that he was dead. He'd blown the back of his head open.

Bella sat a good ten feet from the body, her gaze locked on it.

Ethan called her to him. "Good girl. Come here, Bella."

She trotted toward him and positioned herself behind his right leg.

The commander said, "Could she have killed him?"

"Yes, she definitely could have. I'm not sure she wasn't going to. I think he preferred a bullet over the dog."

"But you said you called her back, correct?" the commander asked. "We can't have killer dogs running around loose."

"Killer dogs, in this case, would be dogs trained to kill," he said gently. "And Bella is not running around loose. As you can see, the victim has no dog bite marks. I wouldn't let her attack him, but he didn't know that. He had already panicked, trying to get the gun into position before she reached him. As it was, she listened to my command just before she got to him."

The men looked at the body, reassured no bite marks were on the man himself. They relaxed. With her at his side, Ethan stepped back another few feet, making more room for the men to maneuver.

"We'll have to take your statement," the commander said, "and verify what you say is exactly what you did."

Ethan didn't say anything.

"Do you live around here?" one of the officers asked.

Ethan shook his head. "No. I'm renting a property close by. It belongs to Gunner Redding."

At Gunner's name, all the officers looked up.

"You know Gunner?"

He gave a slow nod. "And Flynn and Levi and Stone and Logan …" He named a bunch of the other men who lived locally. He could see the relief on the commander's face. He understood. It was one thing to have a complete stranger tell you a story, but quite another thing entirely to tell a story like this and have a half-dozen good men to back him up. If they gave Ethan a good reference, chances were this would go a lot easier. "Feel free to call Gunner if you want."

"And the others?"

He inclined his head. "Of course."

At that, the men turned and studied the dead body, while one of them stepped back and made phone calls.

Ethan shoved his hands into his pockets. "Are you okay if I leave now?"

"Where are you going?"

"Home to check on the animals. I want to drop off Bella there, then go to the hospital."

The commander nodded. "We want your cell phone number and the address where you're staying."

Ethan pulled out a notepad, quickly wrote down his cell phone number, the address where he was staying, and then underneath he added Gunner's name and phone number. He tore off the page and handed it to the sergeant.

The man noted the numbers, folded up the sheet of paper and placed it in his pocket. "We'll be down at the hospital soon too." Then he stopped, turned to one of the men at his side and said, "Daniel, you go with him."

Daniel looked at him in surprise. "You mean, meet him at the hospital?"

The commander shook his head. "Go with him back to his place, check out the address, see what state the dogs are in and then head to the hospital with him."

That made Ethan respect the commander all the more. He was making it clear he didn't trust Ethan, but, at the same time, the commander was willing to give Ethan a chance. He'd contact Gunner and probably Levi, question them whether they knew who Ethan was and what kind of man he was, but the commander was also very concerned about the dogs, whether that was because he didn't want them loose and killing everybody else around them or he was concerned for the dogs' sakes.

Daniel pushed his hat back on his head, studied the commander's face for a moment, then gave a shrug and said to Ethan, "Lead the way."

With Bella at his side, Ethan walked back to his vehicle. "Do you have a cruiser with you?"

Daniel nodded. "But I came with somebody else, so they can take it back."

Ethan led Bella into the truck bed, opened the passenger side for Daniel and said, "Hop in then." He went around to the driver's side, got in and headed up the road.

CHAPTER 8

THERE WAS JUST something about hospitals that Cinn hated. Maybe it was the antiseptic smell. Maybe it was the misery of everybody in the crowded emergency room, with crying children and an old couple who looked like their world had just been decimated.

She looked at Flynn. "I don't need to be here, you know? Isn't there a clinic I can go to?"

He gave a shout of laughter. "If you were an animal, I could take you to Louise. But you're not."

She sagged into her chair. "You know we could die in the waiting room?"

He nodded. "And it's happened," he admitted. "But I'll make sure I get you attention well before that happens."

The trouble was that, although she'd been shot, she wasn't dying. Enough people were here who needed attention ahead of her.

Then her name was called. With Flynn's help, she got up again and was led into a small cubicle. She sank onto the bed with relief. A nurse came in almost immediately. With Flynn explaining what had happened, the nurse cut off her T-shirt, leaving her yoga top underneath unharmed, and took a good look at the wound.

"We'll have to phone the cops," she said. "All bullet wounds must be reported. I'll get the doctor, and he'll examine you."

Leaning against the raised upper portion of the hospital bed, she suddenly felt more tired than she could believe. "Where are my dogs?" she asked.

"I called them before I reached you," he said. "When I saw you with Ethan, I took them back and locked them up in your yard."

She sighed with relief. "I can't believe I didn't even notice."

"The dogs know me," he said. "It wasn't a problem. We needed to get as many variables out of that scene as possible."

She looked up at him and asked, "Did Anna come with you?"

"She went to your place after I told her the dogs were there and stayed to make sure the dogs had food and water and to calm them down."

Cinn nodded. "Thank you."

"I'm sorry I didn't get there sooner," Flynn said. "I was on my way back from town when you called. I started freaking out and called Anna. By the time I got to you, Ethan had everything under control."

"Not only was he there quickly, he went after the shooter," she said in wonder. "I mean, I guess it's not a great outcome for the shooter, but it's the best outcome I could have wished for myself."

"Understood," Flynn said. "At least this way you don't have to look behind you in the dark anymore."

"Exactly. What I don't know is why they targeted me."

Flynn stepped forward, tilted her chin up and glared at her. "Why do you say you were targeted?"

She filled him in on the vehicle parked on the side of the road that came back later in the day. "I don't know if it had something to do with the job Ethan went to help out the cops with."

"Explain," Flynn barked.

She rolled her eyes and gave him as much information as she knew. "I wondered if it had to do with his presence at my place. It's the only reason I can think of for why they went after me."

"But you went for a run. Do you think they followed you?"

She shrugged. "Honestly, I was pretty near the highway for a lot of the run anyway. It wouldn't take much to keep track of me. And I was headed for the tree line, so, if they got there ahead of me, it was pretty easy to take a clean shot."

"Yet they missed."

She wrinkled her nose at him. "I don't think they missed as much as I tripped at the right moment. I had just come over a patch of really uneven ground and caught my foot on a rock and went down. As it was, it caught me in the shoulder instead of higher up, maybe. I don't know. I twisted as I fell, and I didn't move again." She laughed. "He didn't shoot my dogs. They came to me and just stayed there."

"Which is normal behavior for dogs. They'll often stay with a dying owner until either they are rescued or they die themselves."

"That's a terrible thought," she said. "I'd hate to think of the animals sitting beside my cold body, waiting for me to get back up again."

"Dogs are special animals that way. Cats on the other hand ..."

She chuckled. "I love cats, but I have absolutely no illusions. They're very much all about themselves."

He grinned at that.

Just then the doctor walked in. "What's this, young lady? You've been shot?" He poked and prodded her shoulder.

She tried desperately not to cry out, but his touch was not gentle.

"I have to get this X-rayed for any bone breaks," he said. "It looks like it's a fairly clean through-and-through shot. But I can't be sure how much damage might have been done on the way. It looks like you've had a lucky escape though."

He ordered her X-rays and said as he was about to step out, "We have to call the cops."

Flynn was prepared. He handed over a card and told him about Sergeant Mendelsson and the commander they'd met at the crime scene.

The doctor nodded. "Good to know. I'll give these men a call." And he left.

The nurse came in with a wheelchair. They assisted Cinn into the chair, where she was wheeled up to X-ray.

Flynn stayed with her the whole time.

"You can leave, you know?" Cinn said.

He shook his head. "Anna would never let me live it down if I did."

"I'm here. I'm not dying. I'm fine," Cinn stated.

"You aren't fixed up. You haven't been cleared to leave. We don't know if they'll keep you overnight,"

She stayed silent after that. The X-rays were painful but livable. She was wheeled back to the little room in the emergency department, and they waited for the pictures.

Finally the doctor came in and said, "Good news. We'll just stitch you up, give you some shots for the pain and a prescription for more painkillers. You should be good to go home. If you have more bleeding or any problems moving your arm or your fingers, you need to come back in immediately. Do you hear me?"

She nodded. But then she would have said anything to leave. Hospitals were definitely not her favorite place. After she was finally fixed up, stitches in place, the shoulder bandaged and her arm in a sling, it was all she could do to stand up.

Flynn held her other arm. "Are you sure you're good to go home?"

She gave him a tired smile. "I won't rest here. Home sounds much better."

But he didn't appear to be convinced.

"I'll be fine."

"I don't know about that," he said.

Just then another voice entered the room. "She won't be alone, so it's all good."

She turned to see Ethan smiling at her, releasing her hold on Flynn.

He came in, gently put an arm around her good side and gave her a hug. "How are you feeling?" he asked.

"Like I've been shot," she said with a heavy sigh. "The painkiller is kicking in, but it's making me woozy."

"In that case, home to bed with you." He looked at Flynn. "I can take her from here, if you're okay with that."

Flynn glanced at Cinn, then back at Ethan.

Cinn chuckled. "I'm fine, Flynn. It's okay."

"Are you sure?" Flynn asked.

She reached out, gripped his fingers and whispered, "Yes, I'm sure. Feel free to check on me later today or tomorrow morning," she said.

Flynn gave a clipped nod and said, "Count on it." Then he turned and walked away.

With Ethan at her side, she made her way to the front reception area, where she took care of the insurance details, and afterward went outside to the parking lot. There she was helped into Ethan's truck.

As she got in, she looked around, found no sign of Bella. "Where's Bella?"

"She's with the other dogs," Ethan said. He stopped as an officer walked over. She wondered why he was there, but Ethan appeared comfortable with him. As long as nothing else had gone wrong …

The officer went around to Cinn's side. "I came in with Ethan. Are you okay?"

She smiled and nodded. "I will be."

He looked at her, assessing how healthy she was, and then said, "I do need to ask you some questions."

Her heart sank. "Any chance you can do that tomorrow? The doctor gave me a heavy-duty pain shot, and I'm about to fall asleep."

He smiled and said, "I'll be there tomorrow morning." He looked over at Ethan. "Okay, you're good to take her back home."

Ethan hopped in, then turned his head toward the officer. "Do you want us to give you a lift somewhere?"

The officer laughed and shook his head. "No. My ride is on the way."

To Cinn's relief, there were no other delays. Ethan backed up the big truck in the hospital parking lot and took her home.

IT HURT HIM to see her in so much pain. She'd been given a

ETHAN

pain shot, but it either hadn't taken affect yet or wasn't strong enough. That just added to his guilt. It had to be his arrival into her world that got her into trouble. Which meant someone from the drug property had seen him parked close to the property and had followed him back here. That just pissed him off even more. Now he had to find them and stop them. They could not be allowed to get away with shooting an innocent woman. If they wanted to pick a fight with him, then he was all for it. But it needed to be with him and not those he knew.

Especially not someone he was starting to care for. That alone made her special, as his heart had been empty for a long time. When he'd finally found a woman who made him stop in his tracks, like hell he would let anyone else take her away from him.

The question now was, was this over? Had the last man died? Or were there more to take his place?

His vote was, more men would be coming …

So he had to get to them first. The police had already raided the drug base but had obviously missed someone or many someones …

Ethan drove to her house and turned his truck so she was closest to the front door. He put the truck into park, shut off the engine and raced around to her side, opening up the passenger door and helping her out. They could hear the dogs barking inside the house; then suddenly they raced out the doggy door and barked at the side of the house behind the fence.

As soon as they opened the front door, the dogs came barreling inside to greet them. Ethan brushed them back, giving the commands to calm down, but they were as untrained as any dog he'd ever seen.

She crouched, laughing, saying hi to the dogs but keeping herself from getting injured. "Don't even bother trying. I've been gone for too long, and they know I'm hurt, so it only makes sense they need reassurance."

He agreed, and, when she reached up for his hand, he helped her into the living room. "Now do you want to sit down?" he asked quietly. "Or do you want to go up to bed?"

"I'll just sit in the living room for a moment," she said, her voice faint. He watched as she stumbled to the couch. She collapsed and groaned as her shoulder was jolted hard. He gently reached a hand to the side of her cheek. "Take it easy. You're home now."

She nodded. "And damn glad of it too. I'll need painkillers soon."

"Not for a while," he said. "They gave you a shot in the hospital."

She speared him with a look that made him grin. He loved her spunk. She had a temper, and he could appreciate that. She also wasn't shy about letting him know how she felt. Either happy or sad. Also good. She seemed to be balanced, honest and comfortable in her own skin. All good things in his book too. But he really liked the fact that she was full of life and doing something about the injustices in the world. Like her rescue work for the dogs. Sure, she took a lot of criticism for rescuing dogs in other parts of the world, but he'd been there, seen firsthand how bad the dogs had it in war-torn countries. He was happy someone was doing something to help.

Of course, she was easy on the eyes too. Her eyes were not quite a chocolate brown, not quite caramel in color either, but something like a toffee tone with gold flecks. Her lashes were long in a small pixie face, almost a heart shape.

Which made him a fool for noticing. No, just lonely ...

It had been a long time since he'd had a relationship or had even sat down with anybody he cared about. It seemed like he'd become a loner years ago, before he'd started working with the dogs. ... But that had gotten worse after his accident, then losing his parents during his recovery ... Losing Shep, his K9 partner he'd raised and trained for seven years, had been hard and had added a layer of loss. He'd worked with many other dogs, but Shep had been his partner. And they'd both gone into that mission, expecting the worst, and unfortunately this time they got it.

Shep hadn't survived; Ethan had barely survived. Maybe he shouldn't have ...

Still, he had to deal with this nightmare and the woman slowly bringing him back to life.

"How about a cup of tea?" he asked.

She looked up at him gratefully. "That sounds great." She patted the couch beside her, and Burglar hopped up. He snuggled close into her lap, while Midnight jumped up farther down. With both dogs now on the couch beside her, Ethan walked into the kitchen, filled the teakettle with water and put it on. He returned to the living room and said, "I'll take the dogs out in a minute too. They likely need to go."

She made a half murmur, and he took that as an agreement. He whistled for the dogs. They didn't look too eager to leave her, but, when he opened the kitchen door, they came running. He stepped outside and walked them around the yard. She had fenced several acres, so there was lots of space for everyone. He could see the gates where she could have gone out for her run and was torn with the idea of returning to where she'd been shot.

Only he didn't want to leave her alone. He walked

around with the dogs, giving them a few minutes to play and to just calm down and relax after being boxed up for so long. When he found a ball on the ground, he picked it up and tossed it. Burglar took off after it. Midnight followed, so Ethan spent a good ten minutes, just throwing the ball and giving the dogs a chance to run. When he figured the teakettle was ready, he walked back inside to make a cup of tea. He carried the tea to Cinn, surprised to find she was still awake.

"Thank you," she said with a smile. "How are the dogs?"

"They're doing just fine," he said as he held up the cup, still with the tea bag in it. "I couldn't find a teapot. How do you like your tea?"

"A little bit of milk please," she said, "and, if you bring me a saucer, I'll take out the teabag when I'm done."

He put the cup down, went into the kitchen to get the milk. Following her instructions, he added milk to her tea, then returned it to the fridge. Walking back, he placed the saucer within easy reach and sat beside her. "How are you feeling?"

She gave him a lopsided grin that was endearing itself to his heart very quickly. She was small yet valiant. He knew a lot of women would have completely freaked out after getting shot. "I hope it doesn't stop you from wanting to run anymore," he said.

She shook her head. "No, I've always loved to run. I just hadn't expected to get attacked like that."

"Well, I'm glad I got here as fast as I could," he commented. "The last thing I wanted was for you to be a casualty in this war."

"That's what it feels like, doesn't it?"

"It does," he admitted. "The only way they could have

connected you to me is either at the vet or by following me here. And that's only possible if they saw me parked up above their place."

"It's a sad world when we have to worry about being followed."

"Agreed," he said with a faint smile. "And we still have to consider that someone might come after you again."

She stood, and he went to help her, but she waved him away. "I'm going to the bathroom. I'll be fine."

He watched as she slowly shuffled down the hall to the bathroom, the dogs milling around her feet. That was the part of the canine relationship he missed, having the dogs always there, always concerned, always ready for every movement you make. Shep had been the same. Took a step for every step Ethan had taken. They'd been partners all the time, even when at home. A lot of people didn't see who he was on the inside, and he didn't take much time to show anyone. He would only open up with somebody who was special. Cinn had surprised him. Right from the beginning ... He remembered the night he'd dropped by with Chinese food. Maybe he should do that again. She certainly shouldn't be cooking for a few days. "Are you hungry?"

She shook her head as she stood at the bathroom doorway. "No, I'm not. All I need right now is rest." She smiled, adding, "If you're hungry, go ahead and find something. I doubt there's much here, but you can have anything you find."

CHAPTER 9

O N HER WAY back to the couch, much of her bravado slipped away. She managed a few more steps into the living room, where she collapsed onto the cushions. Her two dogs joined her again. She cuddled them the best she could, trying to calm them down, so they didn't jump up and hurt her arm. With the painkillers, she felt better, but, at the same time, she felt weepy and exhausted.

She sat on the couch, her feet tucked under her, so she curled into the corner again, finding that position the most comfortable. One of the dogs stretched out beside her, his head on her legs; the other one lay at her feet. Her sore shoulder was propped up with a pillow, and she just closed her eyes for a moment.

Only a moment ended up being several moments. When she opened them again, Ethan stood in front of her, setting a cup of tea on the small coffee table at her side. She smiled at him. "Is that a second cup? You don't have to look after me."

"No, I don't," he said calmly. "But I want to. And, yes, it's a second cup. Your first went cold."

Warmth flooded through her, filling all the lonely spots inside, something she hadn't felt in a long time. "You're a very nice man."

He gave her a startled look and then chuckled. "You have no idea," he teased. "I could have completely rummaged through your place and stolen all your money, while you were out cold."

"Good luck with that," she said with a smile. "I don't have anything worth stealing."

His gaze warmed in understanding. He looked around at her house. "Is this place yours?"

She nodded. "Yes."

"It's comfy," he said. "I really like that. Coziness is something you miss when you don't have a home base. This is a home, not just a house."

"It is," she said. "You'll find your home base again."

He nodded and sat on the couch at the far side from where she sat. "I will," he said in agreement.

"Where are your dogs?"

"They're all back at the house," he said. He glanced at his watch. "After I have tea and get you something to eat, I'll head out to look after them."

"I don't think I could eat anything," she confessed. "My stomach is pretty queasy."

He frowned and studied her face. "Headache?"

She shook her head, then shuddered as pain racked up and down her spine. "Okay, so there hadn't been a head-ache," she said starkly, "but that movement may have changed things."

"How about just a little bit of soup and a piece of toast?"

She winced. "Honestly, I don't think I could eat any-thing." When he continued to frown at her, she smiled and said, "No point in adding food to a queasy stomach."

"Unless it calms down the stomach and gives the pain-killer something to work on," he said. "I can make you a sandwich."

She lay here, thinking about it, and then said, "Well, if

you made one and left it on the coffee table, then I could have it when I am hungry."

On that note he stood and walked the few steps into the kitchen. She could hear him puttering around, but, since he didn't ask her any questions about what she wanted, she knew it would be whatever came her way. Not that she minded being looked after. It was a novelty she could get used to. She tucked a little deeper into the couch and let the painkillers work.

When she surfaced again, her house was empty. She straightened painfully and saw a note on the coffee table beside a platter of sandwiches. She laughed. "Unless he's joining me, that's way too many sandwiches," she said out loud.

The dogs looked at her and wagged their tails.

"Oh, no you don't," she said with a smile. "Sandwiches are people food, not for dogs."

She reached for the note to see it was from Ethan. She read it out loud. "*I didn't want to awaken you. Sandwiches until morning. I'll call you later.*"

She smiled, made her way to the bathroom, and, after she awkwardly washed her hands, she walked into the kitchen, awkwardly putting on the teakettle. What she really wanted was a cup of comforting tea to have with the sandwiches.

Cinn turned and checked the clock, surprised to see how late it was. She must have slept for several hours.

As she poured milk into her cup of tea, her phone rang. She carefully maneuvered the phone and the teacup out to the living room where she sat on the couch again. "Hello?"

"Hey, you're awake. I was afraid to call earlier, in case I woke you up."

She smiled. "I'm definitely awake. Thanks for the plate of sandwiches."

"Have you eaten?"

"Just sitting down to a cup of tea and having my first bite." She hesitated for a moment, then said, "You made enough for two. Are you coming back?"

"I wasn't sure if you would go to bed and sleep for the night."

"I'm thinking about it," she said, "but maybe, once I get some food in me, I'll be in decent shape for a little while."

"In that case, I might pop by again."

"I'll save you a sandwich."

She carefully placed the phone down and picked up a sandwich. It looked to be ham and cheese. At her first bite, she deemed it excellent. She lifted the corner of the bread to see what gave it the extra special flavor and found a touch of sauce. As she tasted it, she realized it was a mix of mustard, horseradish and mayonnaise. It was really good.

She settled back, happy to relax without crying out in pain. At the hospital, she'd been devastated by the shoulder injury. At the moment though, the painkiller was still taking off the edge, and it wasn't too bad. Of course, if she jerked it or moved it too much, then that was a different story. But, in the sling like it was, she was doing quite well with one hand.

She sipped her tea and waited for Ethan to arrive.

Something about him just made them almost instant friends. It was a little disconcerting. She wasn't the kind of person to step into a relationship as fast as she had stepped into this friendship. Was it a good thing? She trusted him, but she wasn't sure that was smart. She really liked him as a person. It was obvious he had a big heart.

As the headlights turned off the highway and came down her long driveway, she watched uneasily, not sure if it was Ethan or somebody else.

Instinctively she wanted to get up and turn off all the lights in the living room, but it was too late. The truck was only two hundred yards away. Anybody coming down the highway would have caught sight of her well-lit house. With much relief, she watched Ethan hop out of his truck. When he went to lower the tailgate, and a dog hopped down, she thought he'd brought Bella with him.

No. This one was bigger. Darker fur but missing in spots. Scarred?

With the dog on a leash, which was a surprise, he approached the front door, knocked and then stepped in. Instantly her dogs went crazy. She tried to call them back, but they weren't having anything to do with that. Finally Ethan made a sharp whistling sound, and both dogs glared at him, then came back to sit beside her.

She turned to look at the newcomer. It was not Bella. Cinn frowned and shifted back in the couch. "And who's this?"

"His collar says Bart," Ethan said quietly. "He's one of the dogs I rescued from the drug center."

At that, the shepherd swiveled his head to look at Ethan. Then tilted his head to the side.

"Hey, Bart. It will be okay, boy."

The dog slowly lay down on the floor. She wasn't sure he understood what had happened to him, but he was understanding something, ... an absence of abuse probably. "So there were two females and two males, including Sally?"

"Appears to be, yes."

She couldn't take her eyes off the new arrival. The dog

didn't scare her, but a calculating look in his eye made her ever-so-slightly worried. She was used to dogs, but these dogs Ethan kept bringing by were not the kind that made her comfortable to be around. They didn't laze about on the floor like any normal dog.

Bart tracked her movements as if she had something he wanted. And then she realized she was holding a sandwich. In fact, she really did have something he wanted. She carefully replaced the sandwich on the plate, watching as the dog tracked her hand movements there. She grinned. "Did you feed him?"

"Oh, he's been fed," Ethan said. He walked forward, ordering the dog to heel. The dog fell into step behind him.

Surprised, she looked at Ethan, at the dog, and then back at Ethan again. "They're very well trained."

"They *are* very well trained. I just don't know the extent of their training or their loyalty," he said. "I'm still figuring that out."

"I'm not sure how you would do that."

"I'm putting them through their paces. But it's taking some time. I'm working with them one-on-one, so I hope it's okay that I brought this guy." He walked over to the easy chair and sat himself down with Bart at his side. But Bart kept his eyes on the sandwiches.

"Sure." She motioned at the platter and said, "Help yourself."

He leaned forward, picked up a sandwich, and, as he pulled it toward him, Bart made a snap toward it. Instantly Ethan corrected him on it and had the dog lay down until he was calm.

She watched in fascination. Ethan did everything in a controlled, ready manner, as if he was expecting it. "You knew he would lunge for that, didn't you?"

"They were given just enough mistreatment that I figured he had to fight for what he wanted, especially food. A sandwich is an easy test."

"How do you deal with that?"

"He just needs to be corrected every time he steps out of line," Ethan said.

She nodded and continued to watch as Bart tracked the sandwich. With every bite it seemed like Ethan made exaggerated hand movements, moving the sandwich out to where it was obviously visible to the dog; then he would pick it up in a slow motion and take a bite. "Are you teasing him?"

"No," Ethan said. "I'm giving him lots of chances to go for it again."

"He seems to have learned quickly," she said when Bart made no move for the sandwich.

Ethan nodded. "If we were past this kind of training, then I could give him the last bite. But, as it is, I won't take that chance. It's pretty easy to ruin a good dog's training with treats."

She glanced at her two dogs and shrugged. "Mine are spoiled, not that they don't have some training, as they do, but I tend to get lax. Still, they aren't that bad."

"Most dogs are spoiled," Ethan said. "But there's spoiling, and then there's training. You don't dare mix the two."

She wasn't sure she agreed with that, but he was the one dealing with dangerous dogs. She had gentle house pets. She reached for the rest of her sandwich, and Bart's head turned to track her hand. A little unnerved, she settled back and took a bite. "He's not taking his gaze off me."

Ethan nodded and gave a small self-correction on Bart's

leash, and Bart turned his gaze toward Ethan.

She was stunned. "He really is well trained."

"He is," Ethan confirmed. "Almost too well trained. My dogs in the military were this way. Makes me wonder if they've ever had any downtime or playtime. Like people, you can't work all day without repercussions."

She ate quietly for several long moments, studying the dog. "I don't get a sense of animosity from him."

"No," Ethan said quietly. "Attentiveness. He's unsure. He's unsure of me. He's unsure of you."

She smiled. "And maybe that's a good thing."

He reached for another sandwich. His phone rang just then. Instead of picking up another sandwich, he pulled his phone from his pocket.

She listened quietly while he answered.

It was Gunner. It was obvious from the conversation that Gunner had heard about today's events. Ethan looked at her and said, "I'm with her right now, and she's fine. I have one of the dogs with me too."

She could hear an exclamation coming out of the phone.

He just chuckled. "It's fine, Gunner. I know what I'm doing."

They spoke for a few more moments, and he pocketed the phone.

"I gather news traveled fast?"

Ethan nodded, took the sandwich and scarfed it down in several bites. He looked at her and said, "You should be heading to bed soon."

She wanted to shrug, a movement she was only now realizing how often she did by the pain that poked her every time. "I will, after time for the next painkillers." She checked her watch and made a face. "Essentially that's now."

"Do you need help getting undressed?"

She frowned, sat up and thought about it. "No, I think I'm fine. I won't attempt to shower tonight."

"If you want to in the morning, I can come by and change the dressing."

"I think I'm supposed to leave it for a day and then go into the clinic and have them take a look at it."

He nodded and stayed quiet. Finally he stood, ordered the dog to walk with him and said, "Call me in the morning. If you hear anything around the place tonight, you let me know."

She turned to him, accidentally jerking her shoulder. She cried out and clapped a hand on her injury. After a few moments of deep breathing, the greasy waves of pain settled down into her stomach. "Why would you even say that?"

He stared at her with a steady gaze. "You're the one who got shot. And we never did track down the truck."

"Shit. Shit, shit, shit. I forgot about that truck."

"And maybe you should keep forgetting about it," he said. "Enough has gone on today. I doubt any more danger is coming your direction."

"But you don't know that, do you?"

He tilted his head to the side and crossed his arms over his chest. "Are you worried?"

She chewed on her bottom lip as she considered the question. "I wasn't until you brought it up."

"As soon as you lay down, that truck would have popped back into your mind," he said.

She groaned. "Yes, you're right. It would have." She walked carefully to the window and stared up at the highway. She pointed where she'd seen the truck. Of course it wasn't there. "I didn't see it close up, so I couldn't give you details about the driver. It seems like it was the same truck that was back later in the day."

He stood, frowning, thinking for a long moment. "If you want, I can go home, grab a few things, work with the dogs a little bit and then come back. I don't want to be away from the animals too long."

"Not necessary." She smiled. "I'll be fine."

But he wasn't convinced. "I don't like the idea of leaving you here alone."

"It's what we have to do," she said, "because I'm sure as hell not coming to your house. So I'll stay here. You stay there, and it'll be fine."

He thought about it for a moment and said, "I'll come back and check on you tonight."

"I'll be asleep," she warned. "Don't wake me up."

He grinned. "You'll never know I was here."

"If you come into my house, I sure as hell better," she said, "because that would really freak me out. I don't want to wake up with you wandering through my house, scaring the bejesus out of me."

He watched as she headed to the stairs. "I'll take a walk around and check your security."

She made a face at him as she stepped up on the fourth and then the fifth step. "Now you're really scaring me."

"Go take your painkillers, get ready for bed. Have a good night's sleep. I'll make sure you're safe."

With that, she had to be satisfied. She trusted him. No point in second-guessing herself now. He'd been there for her so far. She wasn't about to let nerves change anything. She still had her dogs. They might not be trained guard dogs, but they were great early warning systems.

Upstairs she could hear him walking through the house.

She took off her jeans, leaving on her yoga top, and managed to pull on a clean T-shirt. She did a quick job with a toothbrush, a face wash, and then gratefully sagged into her bed. She took her painkillers and turned out the light. One of the dogs hopped up on the bed beside her, and the other lay on the floor. She didn't hear another sound. She just closed her eyes, rolled over and fell asleep.

ETHAN CHECKED OVER the security on her house. There was only one word to call it—dismal. He didn't like the look of any of it. He pulled a couple windows closed. That would not stop a professional break-in, but it would stop most people. He checked the back door and realized it, too, was Mickey Mouse. He propped up a kitchen chair under the door handle. If nothing else, she'd wake up and would have a chance to escape, if she heard a commotion downstairs.

After doing the best he could, he walked out the front door, locking it shut behind him, and stood on the step for a long moment.

Bart stood at his side, never making a sound, but matched his step pace for pace. He reached out a hand and held it in front of Bart's nose. Bart sniffed it several times, then stared at him. He eased a hand on Bart's forehead, feeling the dog tense at the contact. "It's all right, boy. Your days of being abused are over," he said gently.

He didn't know if the dog understood or not, but he'd like to think that the tone of his voice and his reassuring hand giving pleasure and not pain would go a long way to helping the dog understand. They stood like that for a long moment, as Ethan gently scratched the dog behind the ears and then down the neck.

It would be a long time before he could clip their claws or take the matted hair off their coats. But he'd take every step in the right direction he could. He motioned toward the truck, and the dog hopped into the bed on his own. Ethan closed the tailgate, got into the driver's side, reversed the truck and headed up to the highway.

Once there he parked and got out with the dog and took a look to see if he could spot any tracks. Darkness was settling in, and he had to use the flashlight on his cell phone to check.

There were definitely tracks. The problem was, there were too many of them. Giving up that idea, he hopped back into the truck, allowing the dog in the front of the cab this time. The dog walked over to the far passenger side and stared out the window, but he obediently sat while Ethan drove back to the house.

He didn't like leaving Cinn alone. He figured he'd give himself a couple hours to sleep and then do a quick sweep again of her property, making sure all was well. This way he could change the dogs out at the same time.

Back at his rental house, Ethan let Bart into the house and proceeded to dish out dog food for all four of them. He had Sally segregated. She needed a lot more care.

He still wasn't sure what the relationship was between them. He had her in a spare bedroom down on the main floor. With food in his hand, he walked in, keeping the door closed behind him, and gently checked her dressings. Her tail wagged when she saw him. He crouched in front of her and gently stroked her head. He helped her to straighten up slightly so she could eat. Once she plowed into her food, he realized she was definitely improving.

Nothing like seeing a growing appetite in an injured dog to realize she was well on her way to mending. He sat with her for a long moment.

A dog barked outside the door to the spare room. Opening it, Ethan found Bart looking up at him expectantly. Ethan put a leash on him, then let him inside the room, so he could meet Sally. Her tail went crazy, and she whimpered. The two dogs brushed their noses back and forth. Bart stuck his head into her food and had a few bites, and she didn't seem to care. But then he wanted to sniff her all over. The problem was, she was ill and definitely had that medicine-sick smell. But Bart didn't seem to mind. As soon as he was done sniffing, he found a corner of the blanket and lay down beside her.

Crouching between them, Ethan smiled. "Well, you obviously know each other."

Sally was still tired, and, outside of tail wagging, she kept her movements to a minimum. He needed to get her outside so she could do her business. But that would be a little harder. It was one of the reasons for being in the spare room, because it was closest to the front door.

He dropped Bart's leash and put the sling back on Sally. "Come on. Let's get you out front."

He helped her to the front door, but Bart wanted to come too. So he took Bart's leash dragging behind him, opened the front door and carefully let the two dogs out. Bart wanted to dance and bark around, but, with Sally in the sling, Ethan's hands were already more than full. It was hard to give hand signals.

Carefully, Ethan let Sally walk a few steps in the grass. He was taking the bulk of the weight of her body off her injured leg, while he let her go to the bathroom. He didn't even have bags to collect anything yet. But it was good to see her body functioning normally. After she was done, he helped her walk around the yard once. It was important for her to exercise as much as she could.

He could see she was tiring because he was carrying more and more of her body weight as they made their way back to the front steps. Bart obviously wanted to stay longer. But the front yard wasn't fenced.

Ethan managed to get both dogs back into the house. As soon as he had the front door shut, he dropped Bart's leash and maneuvered Sally back into her bedroom. He helped her lie down again, gave her another blanket to lie on, and then closed the door, leaving her alone. Bart stood in front of the door and whined. But Ethan wasn't sure about leaving Bart with her. He didn't want him to hurt her at this stage of her healing.

"You can see Sally in a little bit, buddy. When we go back in, I'll make sure you get to come and visit too."

Bart barked several times, then lay down in front of the closed door. He just wanted to be close. Ethan figured that was close enough.

Bella was out back. He fed her and gave her several moments of cuddles then brought Bart out to join her. The two appeared to be good friends. Bella had taken to his presence the easiest. He was still a long way from brushing her, but at least she was amiable to having a new owner.

And that was more than he could say for Boris. His name was written in the spikes around his collar. *This* was Ethan's K9:01 dog. His real name was *Sentry*. Ethan quickly sent Badger a text, confirming he had found him.

Sentry still refused to eat. Even with the offer of food, he wouldn't trust Ethan. Sentry didn't bark or snarl when

Ethan approached, but he did back up, and his tail poofed. That was enough warning for Ethan to realize he'd already crossed the line. If he wanted to keep his head intact, he needed to give Sentry lots of reach. He figured, by the time Sentry understood what was going on, he'd already have him where he wanted him. As long as he had the other three dogs' cooperation, it wouldn't take long for Sentry to fall into line. Sentry just had to know it was his idea first.

Ethan walked out to the backyard and stood on the deck, a cup of coffee in his hand as he pondered the night ahead. He hadn't liked the idea of leaving Cinn alone. But he also had the dogs to look after. What he should have done was taken Bella there and left her to guard Cinn. But Ethan didn't know Bella well enough to trust her yet. That she got along with everyone and appeared to listen to the commands as he gave them was one thing, but he couldn't put her in a position where he had to trust her to do the right thing without him being there. He couldn't test her in that way too soon.

Bella was still an animal. That was first and foremost. She'd also been extremely well trained and wasn't as badly abused as the others. Sentry looked to have been systematically beaten into being an aggressive dog. He was the only one that worried Ethan. It could take a long time for him to come around.

As for Sally, well, she looked in pain right now, but Ethan hoped eventually she'd be just as grateful to be with her new clan, safe away from where she'd been.

Ethan checked his watch and found it had been an hour already. He'd planned to go by Cinn's house every two hours. But, once at her place, Ethan figured he'd stick around, see if he noted any suspicious activity, maybe walk the place with the dogs, give them a good run in the dark, do some practice drills and see how they reacted.

As he contemplated the idea more and more, he grabbed Bella and Sentry, leaving the other two behind, putting his selected pair in the truck. Although Sentry was eager to get into the truck, every time Ethan approached, Sentry's lips curled. He would certainly put Ethan to the test.

It was pitch-black outside. Ten minutes later he pulled onto the shoulder of the highway near the edge of Cinn's driveway, just taking a quick look before approaching closer. Then he pulled halfway down her drive and parked. He opened the tailgate, letting both dogs out and hooked Bella up to a leash. Sentry just looked at him. There was almost a dare-you-to attitude in his gaze. Calling him to his side, Ethan closed up the tailgate and walked down the driveway. He surveyed the lack of security on the place and frowned. There wasn't even a gate crossing her driveway. And sure, a gate wouldn't keep the trash out. But it did keep a surprising number of people away.

No lights were on inside Cinn's house. He could hear one of her dogs barking. He let out a gentle whistle to it in reassurance. He walked the perimeter of her yard, getting an idea of what passed for nightlife at her place. With his truck parked halfway up the driveway, he doubted anybody would approach.

He walked out the back gate, where Cinn had gone for her run, took Bella off her leash and told her to run. He picked up the pace, noting the faint path in front of him. The trail was treacherous, particularly when the ground was wet. But Bella appeared to be having a fun time racing ahead, back and forth, and finally Sentry even seemed to relax enough to jump and run around with her.

When Ethan whistled for them, they both came running. Only the look in Sentry's eyes read *What? I wasn't coming because you asked me to.*

Bella fell into step beside Ethan at his command. At that point he put her through several of his regular training paces to see what she knew and what she didn't know. She understood so many commands that he wondered if she was a police dog—or military trained. How likely would that be?

Then Ethan turned to look at Sentry, who shot him another look, this one saying, *Don't even bother.* Ethan ran to the tree line, coming up close to the spot where they'd found the body of the man who killed himself. There he slowed his steps and walked, enjoying the freedom of being out in the moonlight. The moon was high, and it cast a beautiful wide glow across the earth. It gave him a surprising amount of freedom to check out the lay of the land.

How had the shooter known she was out running? Were more drug-house guys watching Cinn's house? Ethan walked out to the highway and turned to look at her house. It was easy to see it off in the distance. If they'd been tracking her, she would have been right there in the open, coming toward them. In fact, she probably ran right into this shooter's range, so he could take her out. But he'd missed.

After Ethan watched for a few minutes, he sauntered back down onto the open fields, looking to see if it was just a lucky position or if this had been planned.

But that also implied forethought. As if the bad guys were hoping she'd come toward them, and the shooter was prepared on the off chance she did. The opportunity had presented itself. He'd have to find out from her if she ran this way on a regular basis. Routine made it much easier to pick off somebody.

He slowly walked back toward her house. As he did, he ran Bella through a few more tasks. She could jump; she was good at walking on her back legs, which really surprised him.

She knew all the basic commands. She knew *go, stop, heel, sit, shake a paw*. And *guard* was a good one because he really liked to see her snap into protective mode with her ears alert. What she had trouble with was relaxing her guard. She did seem to understand *okay*. The command should have been *relax guard*, but Bella didn't understand that command either.

During this testing of Bella's training, Sentry sat and ignored the two of them. Whenever Ethan walked closer, Sentry curled up a lip, but he didn't growl, and he didn't attack. Ethan would take that as progress. He kept walking closer, backing away, and walking closer again, but in casual movements as he worked with Bella, who was all too eager to please. She enjoyed working. She enjoyed the challenges and the physicality of the training.

Ethan could get her to jump up on logs, jump over logs, run flat-out. He hadn't worked on any of the attack signals because he wasn't dressed for it. And he needed to be in a safe surrounding before she went kamikaze on him. She had the ability to take down a man in a heartbeat. He didn't want to be the one who hit the ground with nobody there to help him. And he was a little concerned that Sentry might just jump on that attack bandwagon with a whole lot more glee. At the moment the male dog seemed content to be with them. Or maybe he was content to be with Bella. There was obviously affection between the two of them.

It was good to see that Sentry considered himself the alpha dog here, possibly only because Bart had been injured, but that was where the problem lay because Ethan needed

Sentry to follow Ethan's commands. Still, tonight showed progress. Both dogs responded to commands of *come*, and that was good. Bella responded to *stay* perfectly. Ethan had yet to try it on Sentry.

They sauntered back toward Cinn's house. He knew she was sound asleep, and that was the best thing for her. He had already been out walking for two hours himself.

As he came through the garden and around to the front of the yard, the front door opened, and Cinn stepped out. In a longish T-shirt with some slippers on her feet, rubbing the sleep out of her eyes, she looked absolutely adorable. He took the steps to stand over her.

"I'm sorry if I woke you," he apologized. But inside, he wasn't terribly sorry. He was delighted to see the vision before him.

"I needed to get painkillers anyway," she whispered. She looked down at Bella and smiled. "This is the one you had earlier, isn't it?"

He snapped his fingers and brought Bella toward him. She came over, sat at his feet and looked up at Cinn.

Cinn asked, "May I touch her?"

"Put your hand out, so she can smell you." And then he gave the command to Bella. "*Friend.*"

Bella didn't seem to change her mannerism. But neither was she being difficult. She sniffed Cinn's hand and then unconcerned, stretched out on the porch floor in front of them.

"Well, I guess that's acceptance," Cinn said with a chuckle. She glanced around her front yard. "It's been a long time since I've been outside at this hour of the night."

"It's gorgeous," he said. "We were just out running in the fields where you were shot."

She spun to look at him, her eyebrows rising. "Yes, but I don't have a regular route—nor even make a regular practice of it. I just love to run sometimes. Besides it's good for the dogs. Why?"

He shrugged. "Looking for ways to put Bella through some exercises, and I wanted to keep an eye on the house for a bit, see if any traffic ran along here," he said. "But there's been nothing. It's quieter than I expected, but that's because you are below the highway, so the noise coasts over you."

"That's normal, particularly at this hour. It's really a quiet area," she said. "That's partly why I like it."

He could understand that.

She turned to look at him. "Do you want to come in and have a cup of tea?"

"You should go back to bed," he said gently.

She wrinkled her face up at him and nodded. "I know. But you're here."

"No," he said with a laugh, hopping down the front steps. "I *was* here. But I'm going home now. Go to bed."

"Did you really come just to check on me? I thought you would drive past to make sure nobody parked there."

He smiled. "Nobody has been here recently. And it's already well past two in the morning. I'm pretty sure you'll be fine for the rest of the night."

She nodded. "I'm sure I will." Her dogs swarmed around her ankles, wagging their tails and being generally friendly idiots. Sentry sat on the walkway, ignoring them. She motioned at him. "He doesn't look very friendly."

"He's not," Ethan said. "But that's okay because he's been forced to be a lot of things. Right now it's all about him finding his own way."

Surprised, she looked at Ethan. "I've heard of people

putting all kinds of human attributes on dogs, but I haven't heard any New Age metaphysical ones like you just spouted."

He chuckled. "Hey, my methodologies are hardly New Age. It's all about common sense." He walked toward the truck parked halfway down the driveway, turning to wave at her. "Now go to bed."

She beamed at him. "Thanks for stopping by."

He motioned for Sentry to follow and gave a whistle. Bella came running to his side, and the three walked away.

CHAPTER 10

S HE WATCHED AS Ethan disappeared down the highway. When she had seen him walking around the yard earlier, happy and content, he seemed completely unconcerned about the time of night or where he was. Then why shouldn't he be? He knew he was welcome here. Besides, he *was* part of the night.

Not that he was a predator. More that he was a hunter. And now he had two capable sidekicks to work with him. Although she wasn't at all that sure about Sentry, who looked like he was a whole lot of untamed wolf. Kind of like Ethan. Loners, dangerous, keeping to themselves, and yet, likely to be there when you needed them. At least she hoped Sentry would be that for Ethan.

She slowly made her way back upstairs, grabbed two pain pills from inside the drawer at the side of her bed and swallowed them with water from the glass on the bedside table. On impulse, she got up and walked to the window to take a last look at the night. She wouldn't put it past Ethan to sleep in the truck close by, in which case he might as well have slept on the couch. She had no compunction about keeping him close. He had the protective gene as bad as any male she knew.

That was nice to see in a guy. It had been a couple years since her last relationship. When Jason had walked out, it had been painful and difficult for both of them, but they knew they'd grown as far as they could together. It was time for a change.

She had girlfriends who complained about boyfriends who cheated, boyfriends who lied, and boyfriends who ditched them. It wasn't like that with Jason. They'd sat down, taken a close look at where they were going, what each wanted from life and realized they wanted different things, and really they needed different lives. It had been hard and painful. When he'd walked, he'd walked permanently, and she'd closed the door on that part of her life.

For a while she'd dated, but her heart hadn't been in it. She found that the longer she stayed at home with the dogs, the happier she was. She wasn't antisocial, but neither was she an extrovert who needed people all the time.

As she turned to walk back toward her bed, lights shone into her window. She frowned and watched as a truck took up the same spot where Ethan's truck had been. Instantly her heart hammered against her chest. Would that be Ethan again? Did he just do a circle around and then park again?

She dashed to her night table and grabbed her phone. She sent him a text, asking if that was him again at the top of the driveway.

When she didn't get an immediate response, she walked back over to the window and realized the truck lights were out.

Her phone rang.

"What are you talking about?" he asked without preamble.

"Where are you?"

"Almost home."

"Then you better get your ass back here," she said boldly, "because now a truck is parked at the top of my driveway. And its lights are off."

"Make sure those damn doors are locked," he ordered, his voice terse. "I'll be back in five."

Petrified now, she ran downstairs, holding her injured arm, and found she had indeed left the front door unlocked. She threw the bolt, raced to the back door in the kitchen, saw a chair there and frowned. He must have had a reason for doing that. The garage door was locked.

Nervous, her knees shaking, knowing that, injured as she was, she couldn't fight as hard as she might need to, she made her way back upstairs, where she locked herself in the master bedroom with the dogs and stared out the window from the safety of the curtains, seeing if anybody approached.

She couldn't see anybody, and that worried her too. While she'd been locking the doors, maybe they had made their way down the drive and were outside the house even now. It was an old house with lots of little funky levels and decks and porches. It'd be pretty easy to break in. "Why did I never secure any of that?"

But she answered herself. "Because it's never been an issue before, idiot."

She shook her head as she argued with herself. She had to be really scared to be doing that again. She had talked to herself as a child growing up, and usually only when she was really frustrated. This wasn't frustration. This was something much worse.

Her shoulder throbbed. She wanted to sit down, but she didn't dare leave the window and miss seeing anybody who might be walking toward her.

What she really wanted to witness was Ethan's arrival,

but she saw no sign of another truck approaching. She stood motionless for a good ten minutes, waiting. Nothing.

That's when she heard somebody outside at her kitchen door. She raced to the other window, revealing the back of the house, but couldn't see anything.

With her hand to her throat, her injured arm firmly pressed against her chest, she stood behind her master bedroom door and tried to work on deep breathing. When her phone buzzed in her hand, she opened it to see Ethan was calling. "Somebody's downstairs."

"I know," Ethan said quietly. "I can see him."

"Where are you?" she cried out softly.

"I parked a little farther out and came in the back way. I want to make sure you don't move, okay? Are you in the master bedroom?"

"Yes, I am," she said.

"Good. Stay there. Make sure the door is locked. If somebody comes upstairs or even inside, let me know. Otherwise I only see one person, trying to get into your kitchen door."

"I left your chair there."

"Good," he said, "but it looks like he just went in the window anyway."

She gasped, her heart slamming against her chest. "You'll take him out, right?" Her voice quavered, and she hated that. But the thought of fighting off an intruder terrified her. Already being injured made her feel more unprotected than ever.

"You'll be fine," he said, his voice soothing. "I'm almost there now. Like I said, stay in the bedroom. If you can stop him from coming in, do that. He might ram the door with a shoulder or kick it in with a foot, so don't scream out in surprise."

She glanced around, taking the chair from her small writing table and propped it underneath the bedroom doorknob. If nothing else, the intruder would make a hell of a racket trying to come through. Then she sank to the floor by the door. "Hurry," she whispered. "I've propped a chair underneath the doorknob."

"Good," he said. "Keep thinking. The minute you stop thinking, and fear takes over, you become numb to opportunities you really can't afford to be without."

Her knees tight against her chest, avoiding her injured arm, and her good arm wrapped around her, she sat motionless, waiting. It seemed like forever as she sat curled in a ball, the dogs at her side. But the phone was against her ear just in case Ethan said something. She could hear his breathing. "You've still got the phone line open?"

"Of course," he whispered. "But don't talk if you don't have to. I'm on the way."

Even the dogs appeared frozen. Neither barked nor whimpered. Like her, they understood something was wrong.

She thought she heard something and froze, her breath catching in the back of her throat. Both her dogs were curled up at her side, only the large one bounded to the door, dropped his nose to the edge and sniffed. Instantly Cinn heard heavy sniffing on the other side. She lifted her head, tilted it sideways and wondered.

A knock came. "Cinn, it's me. Ethan."

She bounded to her feet, crying out in pain as her shoulder was wrenched in her quick movement.

"Are you okay?" he asked sharply.

"I'm fine," she said, stumbling to unlock the door.

When she got it unlocked, she pulled it open. Bella jumped into the room, her nose to the ground, and she completely circled the room and came back. Sentry stood at the doorway as if on guard as she checked the place out. Then watched as she played with the other dogs happily.

Ethan wrapped Cinn in his arms and held her close, gently swaying back and forth.

"Did you see him?" she asked. "Did he get away?"

"Yes." He turned and pointed up the highway.

She could see the vehicle was gone. She shook her head. "He was that fast?"

"Maybe he heard me coming," Ethan said. "And he slipped out the front door and took off."

"Really?"

"Or it could have been the dogs. Bella gave a sharp bark, as we came into the house. It might have been in warning, or it might have been in greeting. I don't know."

Cinn turned to look at Bella, who seemed to be happy lying on the floor. Senty still hadn't relaxed. She shook her head. "They're a marvel. But I sure wish we understood them better."

He rubbed her good arm gently, his hand holding her shoulder carefully. "Can you sleep now?"

She shook her head. "No, not now. I'm too wired. When I heard noises inside, I thought it was him coming up the stairs."

He nodded. "I didn't want to give too much warning, just in case he circled back around the house. But he's gone now."

She gave him a wide smile. "Do me a favor? Can you search very, very thoroughly?"

He dropped a light kiss on her forehead and said, "Yes.

And, just to make sure, you come with me, so you can see what I'm doing."

They started with the other bedroom on the top floor. He went through the closets, checked under the bed, behind the door, then led her downstairs so she could check every room with him.

By the time he was done, she was laughing. "Okay, so I made too much out of it."

He stopped in front of her. "Absolutely you did not. That asshat was climbing in the kitchen window. I saw him."

She took a deep breath and let it out slowly. "Right. I keep trying to forget that part."

"Don't," he said, giving her a gentle shake. "Remember he was here. I saw him. It was real. We need to make sure he didn't come with a partner."

"Now that's not a thought I want to contemplate."

"That is definitely a consideration," he said.

She nodded. "It's a grim concept. But I don't know what else to believe."

"I'll stay the rest of the night," he said. "But I want you to get into bed, and I want you to sleep. That shoulder of yours needs to heal."

She grimaced. "It's got to be … What? … Five o'clock in the morning now?"

He checked his watch. "It's not quite quarter to five yet."

She was tired. She leaned against the kitchen counter and brushed the tendrils of hair off her face. Her body was achy and sore. "It feels like I need another painkiller," she muttered.

"That's why you should get into bed and rest. Even getting four hours is huge."

She tried to assess how she felt, but the fatigue was definitely coming on now. "Are you sure you'll stay?"

She hated the fear in her voice. But, after what had just happened, she wondered if she'd ever be comfortable alone again.

"Yes, absolutely I'm staying. Come on. Let's get you back to bed." He walked at her side as she slowly made her way up the stairs. In her room, he pulled back the bedcovers and motioned at her. "Get back in."

She kicked off her slippers and slowly eased herself down.

He covered her up, leaned over, gave her a quick kiss and said, "Now four hours of sleep, nothing less. Do you hear me?"

"Why does it feel so good to finally lie down?"

"Because your body needs it," he said sternly. "I know you can see that highway from where you are, but that's not an issue now. My truck is not up there, and nobody else will be coming back tonight. Understand?"

She gave him a tired smile and waved at him. "Go. I'm fine. I'll be asleep in a few minutes." So saying, she rolled over onto her good side, tucked the pillow up underneath her head and closed her eyes.

He walked across the bedroom and whispered, "Good night."

She listened to his footsteps as he headed down the stairs. She hadn't even realized Bella was with him. But now it was like she was his ghost. Cinn could hear the light padding of Bella's nails as she crossed the top hallway and skittered down the stairs followed by Sentry's more sedate walk. Her own dogs appeared to have accepted Bella like none other. Although they were still wary of Sentry. But then they were used to rescues too. Cinn wondered if she had so easily accepted Ethan for the same reason. Was he a rescue as well? Bella was lost and homeless, a bit of a renegade. No, that was Sentry. Ethan, well, it was hard to find any description for him. But, in a way, he suited the dogs, and the dogs suited him.

The question that occupied her mind as she slowly drifted off to sleep was whether she suited Ethan and whether his whole gang suited hers.

They had something going on between them. She just didn't know what.

As sleep finally overtook her, she realized it didn't matter because she was willing to take the journey and to find out how far they would go. If it entailed two people getting together with a messy load of dogs, well, there were worse ways to live. And, with that, sleep claimed her with a smile on her face.

BACK DOWNSTAIRS, ETHAN stretched out on the couch. He kept a wary eye on Sentry, but Bella just crashed on the floor beside him. She was happy to be with him. Cinn's two dogs were in the bedroom with her. So far, all four animals were getting along, but no doubt the two smaller, happier dogs were giving the others clearance. They were happy to have them around, but they were a little wary. And he could understand that.

He stretched out, rolled over and tried to close his eyes. But his mind buzzed, wondering at the identity of the intruder and why he came here. Ethan should have checked for a license plate. And then he considered something else.

Who would have surveillance of this area? Anyone?

He pulled up Google on his phone to see if anybody might have cameras. Farther down the road was Anna and Flynn's rescue. Did they have anything? Even though it was really early, he sent Flynn a text, asking him. Letting him know an intruder had been on Cinn's property. Following that, he said he chased him off, but he was looking for a black pickup truck, likely a half-ton that had been parked at the top of her driveway.

He fired that off and lay here, thinking about it. Was this connected to him? The only way it could be was if it was connected to the same drug lab they had taken down.

He didn't know for sure, but it was too close a coincidence to ignore. Multiply that with a spy in the sky that could track things like that … But he didn't have access to any of those anymore. That was military-grade surveillance, not something he would pull in on a favor. Cinn had no surveillance and no security to speak of. And that was something he aimed to fix. Soon.

As he lay here, his phone beeped. Surprised, he saw Flynn's name. Flynn was pissed and said he was checking cameras right now.

Ethan responded. **Sorry to wake you.**

Never a better reason than to help a friend.

At that, Ethan settled back with a smile. He wasn't sure if Flynn meant that Cinn was a friend or that Ethan was. Either way, it was good they had somebody on their side.

Suddenly Sentry bolted to his feet, his hackles rising as he stared at the kitchen. Ethan hopped to his feet and glided across the living room floor, pulling up against the wall just short of the doorway.

That had been the other concern he'd had, that there

might have been two men—one who took off in the truck and the other sticking around. Ethan's truck was parked farther up the highway, out of sight. But did anybody know he was still here? He could hear something rattling at the kitchen door. He sent Flynn another text, then pocketed his phone, crouching down low.

When people came in, they rarely looked down at floor height. Once again, Sentry growled deep in the back of his throat. Ethan studied the dog. That anger, the full fluffed-out tail and hunched shoulders. Ethan wasn't sure if it was the man arriving who was setting off Sentry or the fact that it was *any* intruder at the house.

Sentry was obviously a guard dog, but was he guarding the house, or did he know the person coming toward him and hated him?

Both were possibilities, giving Ethan lots to work from. But he couldn't count on the fact that Sentry would follow Ethan's instructions. Bella, on the other hand, was now positioned right beside him, same height as he was, nudging him, her tail wagging. He studied her for a moment, as he heard the rattling at the door. Whoever it was trying to get in was shitty with a pick. And that was something he filed away.

He reached out a hand and placed it on Bella's muzzle. She quieted, her tail stilled, and she lowered her head to her paws, ears forward. He smiled. You had to love a dog that could pick up the nuances like she did.

Suddenly the door popped open. For a moment there was nothing. Ethan watched from down low as a man dressed all in black with a hood over his head stepped into the kitchen. He glanced around, as if familiarizing himself with the layout, then quickly moved toward Ethan.

Ethan held back Bella, but Sentry wasn't being held back at all. He snarled and growled audibly.

The man froze, reached out a hand. "Boris?"

Sentry froze, his nose wrinkling, but the deep growl resumed. Instead of running away, the intruder stopped, raised his hand in a stop command for Sentry and then, in a harsh whisper, ordered him to stand down.

Sentry slowly stood down, his training taking over at a voice he recognized. Ethan watched carefully because Sentry, although he was giving way, didn't like it. He was looking for an opportunity to move on his own.

The intruder walked forward a few steps. "Good boy. I was hoping you would be around." As he crept closer, talking calmly to Sentry, the dog growled again in the back of his throat. The man held up his hand. "What's wrong with you, Boris? You know better than this." He stopped a few feet away from the open doorway as his gaze caught sight of Bella. "Bella?"

Bella didn't growl or bark. She stared at him, her ears back and her teeth showing.

That confirmed an awful lot for Ethan. They both knew him. Neither wanted anything to do with him.

The man slowly reached around behind him and pulled out a leash and a rope. He also had what appeared to be a police-issue baton. At the sight of the baton, Sentry growled louder. The man tucked it behind his back. Sentry calmed slightly but not enough.

So the baton was the intruder's weapon of choice.

And the man had come prepared for these dogs.

Well, this asshole had had his last opportunity to beat up these dogs. Ethan waited for the man, leash in his hand, as he crept closer to Bella.

"Bella, you're looking good. Can you sit up for me please?"

Bella stayed down, her head flat on her paws as Ethan had told her, her ears back. The man with the leash started to crouch, to get close, and her lips curled even higher, and in the back of her throat was her first warning sound.

The man stared at her. "What the fuck? Why are both of you being such pains in the ass right now? What the hell happened to you?"

Ethan wanted to punch him flat in the face and let the dogs have at him. But the man wasn't quite close enough yet. Ethan couldn't be sure another weapon wasn't somewhere on the asshole. But, if Ethan got a chance to grab that baton, he'd take a few good wales on the asshole.

The man reached out a hand to Bella. She didn't move, but she growled. He froze, then ordered her to obey. His voice rose, although still quiet enough not to wake anybody else in the house. His tone was sharp, getting angry.

At that, Sentry stood and approached. His ears flat, his teeth showing, he growled at the intruder.

The man froze. "What the fuck has happened to you, Boris?" He took one more step forward, and it was enough.

Ethan snapped around the corner, his right hand out, connecting hard with the man's nose and jaw. He never even saw it coming. The blow was hard enough to send him backward several flailing steps before he went down on his back.

Sentry went after him.

The man cried out, again reaching for the baton, as Sentry grabbed the intruder's arm and stood over him. He shook the man's wrist, almost as if seeing the baton as an extension of the arm.

Bella still lay here at Ethan's command.

Blood running down the intruder's arm, he screamed at Sentry, but Sentry wasn't listening. He shook the intruder's arm harder, his jaws crunching on the man's weak forearm. The baton flailed around as the man tried to use it to get at the dog.

Ethan stood, stepping on the man's other arm, and said, "Drop the baton. If you don't, I'll let him take off your arm."

The intruder stared up at him. "Who the fuck are you? If you're the asshole who ruined our dogs, I'll make you pay for that," And then he screamed again as Sentry clenched down tighter.

"Apparently somebody the dogs prefer over you." Ethan grabbed the baton carefully, so as not to let Sentry see it as an extension of *his* arm, and said, "Let go."

The man really had no choice as Sentry once again shook hard. The intruder's fingers opened, and the baton dropped to the man's chest. Sentry saw it, released the man's arm and lunged for the baton. Ethan let him have it. He let him take the baton away and start to destroy it.

Ethan crouched beside the injured man and said, "What the hell did you do to that poor dog?" He pulled off the man's face mask, exposing the intruder. Ethan didn't recognize him.

"Are you the one who ruined our dogs?" the man roared.

He tried to attack Ethan, but, with Ethan stepping on his good arm, and his injured arm bleeding profusely, there wasn't a whole lot he could do except to kick his legs. As soon as one leg came up, Ethan grabbed it and pinned it down. The man screamed again.

Bella moved closer. Ethan looked at her and said,

"Good, Bella."

She looked up at him, then looked down at the intruder, but her stance didn't release.

"The dogs really hate you," Ethan said, "if even now, when they have an opportunity to turn on me, they don't want to."

"They will," the man said. He snapped out commands at Bella to *attack* and *kill*.

Bella, confused, obviously upset at the sight, stared at Ethan.

He kept murmuring to her in a gentle voice, "Relax, Bella. Just *guard*. Nobody kills anymore."

The man on the ground lost his temper, shouting and hurling epithets at her.

At this point she looked at Ethan and sat down on guard duty. He smiled. "You see? You can't lose your temper with an animal. And you can never take it out on them with a weapon," he said in a conversational voice. "You can't rule by fear."

"It's the only way you do rule," the intruder snapped. He groaned. "He broke my arm."

"Yeah, he might have," Ethan said. "But that's not my fault. You were breaking and entering into this house."

The man glared at him.

His arm bled badly enough that Ethan knew he had to put a stop to it. He noticed a tea towel tossed against the back of a kitchen chair. He looked at Bella, looked at the tea towel, pointed and said, "Bella, fetch."

She bounded to her feet, looked at him in confusion. He pointed at the tea towel, and she wandered in that direction, sniffed, looking for something to fetch, and he said, "Higher." Her nose went up a little bit higher. She grabbed the tea towel and brought it to him but obviously was not certain of her position.

He grabbed it, smiled and gave her a gentle pat. Then he praised her. "Good girl, Bella. Good girl. Now go back and *guard*."

She returned to her position and sat down to watch the intruder.

Ethan ripped a strip off the tea towel and wrapped it around the intruder's wrist, putting pressure on it to stop the bleeding.

"I need a hospital, damn you," the man cried out. "Not some backward medicine."

"What you need is a bullet," Ethan said calmly. "And, of course, if Sentry had killed you in the meantime, I certainly wouldn't have had a problem with that."

The man glared up at him.

Ethan said, "How many people have you had these dogs kill?"

The man sneered. But the waves of pain were taking their toll on him.

"They're just animals. And Boris is my number one tracker. But he's nowhere near what my Billy was."

"What happened to this Billy?"

"He was shot after he killed a man during a fight. Another guy got out a gun and shot him, but Billy got his man anyway. Unfortunately we had to put him down."

"And how many men had Billy killed?"

The intruder shrugged. "Maybe a dozen. I don't know."

"And Boris?" Ethan asked, using the name the intruder used.

"He's attacked many, but I don't think he's got any kills under his belt yet. But he's young. By the time he's six, he'll be well seasoned."

"Not if I have any say in the matter," Ethan said cheerfully. "An animal like that, which gives you his loyalty, and all you do is turn him into a killer."

"That's why he was loyal. His predecessor loved the taste of blood. Don't kid yourself. These animals love an opportunity to take something down and tear it to shreds."

They both looked at Sentry, who even now had the baton in shreds of leather and padding. But he was still working off his temper, still growling and attacking it. As Ethan watched, Sentry calmed slightly and focused on ripping off every piece of fabric and leather on the heavy steel center.

Ethan shook his head. "It's good therapy, isn't it, Sentry?"

"Good therapy is giving him a bloody cat or a rabbit to eat, preferably still alive," the man snarled. "You're ruining these dogs. And you've got a hell of a nerve stealing these animals and changing Boris's name. We all worked them and hard to get them to be the way we wanted them, and you are messing them up."

"It's not your problem anymore," Ethan said. "You'll go away for a long time."

"For what?" the man sneered. "For breaking into my girlfriend's house because she was having a little snit fit? Obviously she changed the locks, and I didn't know about it."

"It's not that simple," Ethan said. "You're connected to the dogs. That puts you in the drug operation."

"What do you know about the drug operation?" the man asked, his voice hesitant.

"More than you do," Ethan said. He could hear a vehicle

approach. He wasn't sure who it was, but he hoped it was Flynn. He needed back up soon. This asshole, as much as Ethan didn't want to get it for him, needed medical attention. Ethan was of the opinion a six-foot-deep hole out in the back would have been a perfect answer. But rough justice had gone out of Texas a long time ago. Too damn bad.

"You can't know anything about it. That place has been operating in the shadows for a long time."

Ethan nodded. "So true. Until she told me all about it," he added with a smile. "Once I heard about it, then I couldn't leave it alone." He could see the confusion in the intruder's eyes.

"Her? What are you talking about?"

But Ethan decided not to share. "Besides, it's shut down now."

"Yeah, but it'll only grow," the guy said. "It's not like you'll hit them hard enough to stop them."

"If you want to share that information with the police, they might let you off a little lighter."

"Not likely. I'll get killed in jail anyway," he said. "The bosses went through a bad patch a while ago. They should have killed off any loose ends. It would have saved them a lot of pain and money. Now it's standard practice after that mess."

"Quite possibly," Ethan said. "And I can tell you one thing, if you ever come back here, I'll kill you myself."

The man glared up at him, then he said in a low voice, "I still don't understand what woman you're talking about."

"And I won't tell you," Ethan said. Hearing footsteps at the front door, Ethan slipped back slightly out of view. A heavy knock came at the door. "Flynn?"

"Yeah, it's me. You okay here?"

"Come on to the kitchen door. Turn on some lights. This asshole is bleeding all over the floor."

As Flynn approached, Sentry stood, growling in the back of his throat. Flynn stopped in the doorway and put up his hands.

Ethan said, "Hit the light switch."

Flynn followed his instructions. Light flooded the living room so Ethan could see Sentry with his haunches up, standing over the absolutely destroyed baton. But it also showed Ethan beside a man bleeding quite badly on the floor.

Flynn's eyebrows rose. "Is she still asleep or is she upstairs hiding?"

"Believe it or not I think she's asleep."

Flynn looked at the dog in front of him and said, "This must be one of those big rescues you took on."

"It is. This is Sentry." Ethan let out a sharp noise, then said, "Sentry, Flynn is a *friend*."

Sentry wasn't listening.

"Sentry, *stand down*."

Sentry gave a hard shake.

Ethan looked at the smirking intruder. "You think it's funny you created a dog that's a killer?" He motioned at Bella. "Bella, *stand guard*." And then Ethan slowly straightened and walked over to Sentry, who stood in front of Flynn. Ethan walked up beside Flynn and stood at his side.

Sentry looked at Ethan and then back at Flynn.

Ethan reached down a hand, put it on the dog's fur, reached out his other hand toward Flynn and said, "Give me your hand." He did so, and Ethan told Sentry in a firm voice, "*Friend. Stand down.*" His voice brooked no argument, but it was also calm and orderly.

Sentry slowly quieted, the hairs on the back of his neck easing down as he studied the new arrival.

Flynn brushed his hair off his forehead and said, "Wow."

"It should be safe for you to approach."

Flynn looked beyond them into the kitchen and said, "Good thing because your intruder's trying to escape out the door."

Ethan turned and saw the guy getting to his feet to make it to the kitchen door. "Bella, *attack*," he ordered.

Bella spun and jumped on the intruder's back, clamping down on his shoulder, bringing the man to the floor again.

Ethan walked around Sentry, who was already heading toward Bella, looking for some fun himself.

In the kitchen, Ethan ordered both dogs to stand back, which they did surprisingly enough. He grabbed the intruder, slammed him onto a chair and asked, "Do you want to go for another round?"

By now his shoulder welled up with blood too. He stared up at the two men, pain glazing his eyes.

Ethan turned to look at Flynn and said, "Do you want to call the cops for me?"

"I already did," he said. "I figured that, if you had an intruder, you probably would take them down, and we'd need the cops eventually."

Ethan checked the intruder's shoulder. "You'll be fine," he snapped.

"I'll fucking shoot the dogs," the intruder said. "You just wait. I'll get another chance, and I'll take them both out."

Sentry lunged forward as if understanding what the intruder had said.

Ethan held up his hand and ordered Sentry to stop. He didn't look like he would for a long moment. With his growling up the back of his throat and his hackles raised, Ethan stood strong. But he didn't use force.

Finally Sentry calmed down. As if giving the intruder a disgusted look, Sentry gave his head a shake and turned to join Bella sitting off to the side.

Flynn approached quietly. "Are you sure he's safe to have around?"

"He'll be the best damn guard dog anybody could want," Ethan said. "But we have to let him know most people aren't mean assholes, like this guy."

"If you say so."

Ethan laughed and sat on the floor between the dogs. He reached up to scratch them under the chin.

Flynn stared in astonishment. "You're braver than I am. How did you know they would let you do that?"

"Both dogs are good animals," he said quietly. "They will take to affection as much as they're running away from the brutality of this asshole."

"They're our dogs, and you're ruining them," the intruder roared. "I came to get them back, not sit here and watch you destroy them."

"Oh, interesting," Ethan said. "I thought you might have been here for other reasons. Regardless, you'll be disappointed on both counts." He tilted his head to the side and studied the man. And then looked at Flynn. "What am I missing?"

But Flynn's face had shifted and had locked down into a much harder, colder man than the one who had first arrived. He stepped backward, flattening against the wall as he sidled up to the window. "Did you have a chance to see if this guy came alone?"

Ethan froze. Then he hopped to his feet and moved forward. "Bella," he ordered, "with me." At the bottom of the stairs he turned to look at Sentry and said, "Sentry, *guard.*"

Sentry snapped to attention, his ears up, and returned to the intruder on the chair.

Ethan ran up the stairs with Bella, wondering if this had all been a distraction, and he'd missed the main event. Knowing he would wake her and terrify her, he shouldered open the barricaded door and stepped in regardless. With his heart in his throat, he stared at the empty bed, his worst thoughts confirmed. Bella raced forward and searched, but she ended up at the window. The window beside a door that led to a deck with a nice set of stairs down the back to the bottom deck.

Somebody had kidnapped Cinn.

CHAPTER 11

HE PAIN WOKE Cinn first. She moaned. Feeling her head pound, she rolled over onto her side, curling up into a fetal position, her hands clutching her temples. When she felt something wet and sticky, she pulled her fingers away and slowly opened her eyes. Her lids were heavy, as if she'd been crying nonstop. Her body throbbed, achy, but it was her head and her bloodstained fingers that were her main concern.

Her hands were free but she was lying on the floor in what appeared to be an empty room. A ramshackle room. There was a door but no windows that she could see. The area was small, maybe a ten-by-ten-foot space. There was enough light to see she was into a new day, yet still early.

What the hell?

Not sure what had happened, she propped herself on her right elbow, then cried out at the pounding in her head. She collapsed back down, gasping for breath, shuddering as her shoulder took the force.

Her shoulder throbbed. Slowly memories filled in the blanks in her mind.

Ethan had sent her back to bed. She lay here, frowning as the memories filtered back in. If this had happened to her, what had happened to Ethan? She was pretty damn sure he'd have been a hell of a watchdog. For her to be here now, something calamitous had to have happened to him.

She rolled over gently, trying not to cry out in pain. Between her head and her shoulder, she was mess. Where was she? Was she truly alone? Or were more assholes waiting outside for her?

The door was to her right. Moving gently so as not to further jar any of her injuries, she leaned on the wall beside the door. She reached up with one hand and tried the knob. It was not locked. She frowned, wondering if it could be that easy. Using the door for support she slowly made her way upright.

Once stable, she leaned against the wall for several moments as her breathing calmed. She listened through the crack in the door but heard nothing on the other side. Frowning, she pulled the door open enough that she could stick her head out—finding herself in a shed in the middle of a large property. But she noted other sheds were here too. This made no sense at all.

A larger building stood in front of her. She didn't recognize the area. She didn't recognize the buildings. She had absolutely no clue where she was. But she hadn't come on her own. Those people had to be around somewhere. She had to get out of here, and she had to get out fast. She crept around to the back of her shed and surveyed her options. A fence was ahead of her, but it had rolled barbed wire over the top as a major deterrent. Not to mention it could be electric. She'd only find out the hard way.

The fence appeared to go all the way around on all three sides she could see of the property. She moved to the left side of the shed and still couldn't see another way out. What were the chances this was a compound, and she was caged inside with just the one escape route? Maybe, with her injured arm and head, she could climb up to the barbed wire, but she wouldn't make her way through the big coils at the top.

Moving as fast as she could, she slipped over to the next shed to get a better view of what was on the other side. She peered around the corner to see a road and a gate. She tapped on the shed behind her, wondering if anybody was there. She didn't hear anything. She found a slight hole in one of the wooden planks. She lowered to her knees and whispered. With no answer and not seeing anything through the odd knot in the wallboard, she wondered if the other sheds in the area were empty. Then she caught sight of something hanging.

She peered at different angles, trying to look up, but couldn't see what it was. It appeared to be plants drying. She straightened slowly, studied the area around her, wondering if she was on the drug property that Ethan had worked to bring down. In a twisted way it made sense. And notched her panic up that much higher. She needed to get the hell out of here. But there didn't appear to be any breaks in the fence or any spot where she could slide under. Then she reconsidered that. Directly behind her, along one of the fence posts, was a little bit of a hollow, with rocks filling the gap.

Could she stay hidden long enough to clear that hollow enough for her to get under? She wasn't very big. She crept over, crouched down flat and started removing the rocks.

As soon as she thought she had enough room, she flattened and scooted under headfirst. By the time she got her hips through on the other side, she could feel her panic choking her. Finally she'd managed to scrape her way to her feet, and then bolted as fast as she could away from the fence.

Every step made her want to cry out, but the fear of getting caught won over her pain.

There was a rise ahead of her. She climbed it, her heart pounding hard inside her chest. She crested the rise, skidding down the first few feet on the other side. There she came to a stop amid the dust. All she could see was more of the same. Sand, rocks, tumbleweeds even. There was vegetation, but it was wild, unkempt, uncultivated. All around her was miles of raw land.

She stared in awe at the vastness, wondering how the hell she was supposed to know which way to go.

The smart thing to do would be to follow the road. But it was also likely a way to bring her in contact with somebody she didn't want to see. If she could keep the road in sight, she could follow it from a distance. It had to lead somewhere.

With that thought uppermost in mind, she crept up to the next rise, so she could study the property below. It was large, fenced, secure and very private.

If it was the drug property, it was also the same property Ethan had collected the dogs from. She searched for her phone, but of course she didn't have it. Neither did she have much in the way of clothing. She was wearing a long T-shirt, of all things. And bare feet.

She stared down at her bleeding feet in bemusement. She hadn't even considered that. She was out here in the middle of nowhere in the thinnest clothing possible, with nothing to protect her feet, not even socks. "Shit. Shit. Shit."

And she had no way to contact Ethan. He was definitely the one she needed to call. She considered returning to the shed to see if anything would make her walk a little bit easier. Shoes? Water? A cell phone? But she was afraid she'd run out of luck and get caught. She turned to study the miles of rough land around her.

Once the sun rose higher, her feet would burn in the sand too.

Keeping just under the rise, so nobody could see her, she moved in the direction of the road. The rise dipped down, almost flattening up ahead as it came along the road.

Grimly she pressed on. Time was of the essence. Had these men replaced the dogs Ethan had taken? If they had, the dogs would find her in no time.

Moving as fast as she dared, she kept going until she could see the driveway turning away from the property, heading toward town.

About a half hour later she had to sit down, gasping for breath. Not only was her head booming again but the pain of her feet now added to it. With all the jerking and slipping and sliding in the rocks, her shoulder was on fire. Oh, for a sling. Even worse she'd barely covered any ground. The property was still in sight. Thankfully she saw no sign of anyone. She figured, if she did see any strangers, it had to be the men who had kidnapped her. Her head throbbed at that thought. *They must have hit me, knocked me out, then taken me here.*

Grimly she searched over the rise to see if there was any activity at the property. But she couldn't even see a vehicle, which surprised her. Had she been dumped here and left alone, not one guard on duty? If so, when were they returning?

She was just coming around to the side where the front gate was. She was tempted to go into the guard house and see if she could call for help. But who would she find there? Was it suicide contemplating doing that?

Making a sudden decision, she crossed over the rise and

skidded down the far side, swearing at the pain that rubbed against her feet and opened a million little slices along her soles. She hit the driveway and kept going until she saw what appeared to be a huge building ahead of her. But instead of going in the front, she headed around to the back.

There wasn't a sound. It was like a ghost town. But then she remembered what the cops had done here, so maybe no one was left.

There was a door. Hesitantly she reached for it. When the knob turned under her hand and the door opened, she stepped inside, loving the cool air. She crept into what appeared to be a large open room with several smaller rooms behind it. There were no lights on, no sounds. The place appeared to be empty.

She did a quick search and found no one. Then she did a closer search, looking for anything she could use. An old water bottle was on the floor. She snatched that up. Now all she needed was water. Continuing to check, she found a pair of socks tossed into a corner, a big hole at the heel of one of them. She didn't care; her feet would be only half as big as the person who had worn these socks.

She carefully placed them on her feet, almost crying out in relief at the soft padding. She put weight on her feet again. That was an improvement. Now all she needed were boots, water and a phone, but she couldn't find anything.

Back in the main room again, she checked what appeared to be a desk and found a cell phone. But it was dead. She popped out the battery and left it on the desk for a moment. Had it been left behind in the chaos with the police?

She knew, if she gave the battery a moment before putting it back in again, she might get a few seconds. Maybe enough to get a call through—if there was any cell service out here.

Hey, she'd try anything. She popped the battery back in, her mind working as to who to call. It would be tough to get 9-1-1. They asked so many questions she'd have no time. She hadn't memorized Ethan's number. How about her own? She dialed her phone and waited. When the voicemail kicked in, she gave a quick report as to where she was and what had happened. Just as she finished, the phone died.

She stared at it in her hand and then pocketed it. She didn't know who it belonged to. But, if it had anything to do with this place, maybe the police could do something with it.

She wandered the rest of the huge compound, looking for anything that could help her. She did find a small kitchen and running water in the main building. Thirstily, she drank her fill and then filled her bottle. Even if she could locate a bicycle, that would help. She did find shoes, but they were too big to keep on her feet. Other than that, she was pretty well done here.

With a final look around, she headed to the entranceway to the property. Just then she saw a plume of dust in the distance. She scampered up the side of the rise again and disappeared over the edge. Had she made it before they saw her?

The vehicle sped in and hit the brakes. As it came to a stop, she heard doors opening and then more doors opening.

She winced, picked up her feet and started to run. The socks helped a lot. Her feet were sore, but worse than that was the option of getting caught by these guys. Not again. She had very little choices of places to hide. But she'd seen where the plume of dust had come from and knew the general direction that the road would go.

She headed off cross-country toward the road. She just had to stay out of sight. She knew she didn't have much time. Five to ten minutes at the most. Then they'd be all over the place, searching for her. When that happened, she would be in deep shit.

HEARING THE PHONE ring, Ethan ran back into Cinn's bedroom. He'd been searching the top floor, looking for anything. Her phone on the night table continued to ring. Just as he got to it, it stopped. He picked it up, unlocked it and listened as the phone said he had one voicemail. *To hear the voicemail, press 11.*

He pressed 11 and heard Cinn's voice. His blood ran cold. When the message was cut off, he wasn't sure what to think. Had the phone died? Or had she been captured? Or had she been forced to say that to lure him into a trap? Not that it mattered because he was obviously going. He ran downstairs to tell Flynn. His voice terse, he explained the message.

Ethan pulled out his own phone and called Levi. "I'm heading home to get my gear and switch out the dogs," he called out, running to his truck.

"I'll track your GPS and follow you," Flynn called after him, "as soon as the cops arrive to take this asshole off my hands."

At home, Ethan freed Sentry and Bella from the truck bed, figuring out the best plan for this rescue. They all fast-walked straight through to the backyard, Sentry and Bella at his side. Sally barked inside, wanting to join them. But it was too soon for her. Bart had been outside in the fenced-in backyard all this time and came toward Ethan. He frowned, not sure he could handle all three. Sentry, of course, was the wild card. Maybe Ethan would leave him behind this time.

Grabbing Bart and Bella, securing Sentry inside the fence, Ethan returned to the truck, put both dogs into the bed, grabbed his SAR vest and turned around to see Flynn standing right behind him. "How did you get away so fast from the cops and their questioning?"

Flynn smirked. "Told them that you were nearby in state land, and I would grab you real quick for them." At that, Flynn laughed. "They didn't leave our bad guy to follow me. … We'll explain later when we have more time."

"*Humph,*" was all Ethan murmured, but his expression said, *Good job.*

"What are you going to do?" Flynn asked as he followed Ethan to enter his rental property.

"I'm going after her," Ethan said. "I know the property, where the drug bust was earlier. There's a way to get in under the electric fence, if we want to try that way in."

"I thought the police cleaned out that place?"

"They did," Ethan said tersely. "That doesn't mean the drug runners didn't move back in. Obviously she thinks that's where she is, so I have to go find out."

"If she got free, she could be anywhere around the countryside," Flynn said.

"I know. That's why I have the dogs."

"You should take Sentry too," Flynn said.

"Why is that?"

"Because these men have guns. They can take out the dogs. But the more dogs there are, the harder it will be for them to shoot them all."

Ethan considered that, then nodded. "You have a point.

Still two are enough to handle. Although Sentry might be the better tracker in this instance. Let me grab a medical kit, ropes and more water." He changed his shoes for hiking boots and then grabbed his emergency supplies vest—the one from his truck, the one he'd used on search-and-rescue so often, yet not in the last several years. Then he walked into the kitchen and filled the water bottles from his vest. There was no way to know how badly hurt she was or how dehydrated.

His mind raced through the possibilities of what he would need. He moved with the same care he was known for. He'd done this type of rescue many, many times. What he didn't have was weapons. He turned to look at Flynn. "I need a weapon."

Flynn raised an eyebrow. Then he nodded. "I have a piece in the truck." He disappeared.

Ethan packed up and loaded the rest of the gear he needed in the front of the truck. Sentry understood something was going on, and he was being excluded. He bucked like a crazy man, trying to jump up and over the fence. Ethan came back with a heavy leash and stepped out into the back door.

Sentry ran toward him. But first they had to come to a meeting of minds. Ethan stood there, arms crossed, leash in his hand as Sentry tried to get past him. Sentry growled and howled and kicked up a fuss. He really did not like to be left behind. Then Ethan held out his hand with the leash. "Sit."

Sentry stared at him, but his butt went down, and his head went up. Ethan clipped on the leash, told him to heel and then walked him through the house, out to the back of the truck. He opened the tailgate and let the dog jump in to join the others, then moved Bart into the backyard. "Not this time, boy."

Now with two dogs aboard, Ethan went to the front of the truck. He should have a big suburban to carry the dogs or at least a canopy on his truck to keep them safe.

Flynn walked toward them, talking on the phone. He handed Ethan a small handgun, service-issue, and several clips. "I'm coming behind you," he said. "Levi is on his way as well."

"Tell him to contact Sergeant Mendelsson," Ethan said. "He's the man I was with yesterday morning."

Flynn nodded. "Will do. Remember. You're not alone anymore, dude." And he turned and hopped into his truck.

While Ethan watched, Flynn did a quick turnaround, taking off to the left. Ethan drove up to the highway and took a right. He might not be alone anymore, but he sure as hell didn't understand exactly what he did have. Things had gone from slow to top speed in no time. And poor Cinn had been caught in the middle.

Just like the dogs had been.

Ethan had taken on a lot all at once. But he realized, as he headed out toward the countryside where she was probably on the run, he was the best person to find her.

Both dogs knew her scent, as Ethan had remembered to grab the jacket that she had been wearing the day before. She'd worn it to the hospital, carefully draped on her shoulders, and, even better, it had some of her blood on it. If the dogs could find her, they would.

Ethan drove to where he had parked last time. He pulled the truck into the hollows behind a rise so it couldn't be seen, or at least he thought it couldn't be seen. Considering somebody had tracked him back to Cinn's place, he wasn't so sure about that now. He hopped out as his phone rang.

"Ethan," he said, his voice terse.

"Ethan, it's Levi. We have a team of four men coming in your direction. I need you to stay in contact with them."

"I've just parked. I'm unloading the dogs now."

"Is that wise?"

"This is what I do," Ethan said. "The dogs will track her in no time."

"But will they save her, or will they take her out?" Levi asked, his voice worried.

"Good question," Ethan said. "I guess this is a good trial. If I have to, I'll kill them. But it's not what I want to do."

"You could also be going up against more of their trainee dogs."

"That could be both good and bad," Ethan said. "Don't forget. These animals were abused."

"Oh, I remember. That's why I'm worried. Go get her," Levi said, his voice calm and steady. "We'll be right behind you."

CHAPTER 12

S HE DIDN'T KNOW when the pain and the lack of oxygen took over. But she was on autopilot, just moving one step to the next step. Somewhere along the line she realized anybody driving on the road would see her now. The ridge was long gone; it was just flat cross-country terrain. She approached a bend in the road up ahead. She didn't know if that was a good or bad thing. She twisted behind her to see a vehicle driving toward her, dust billowing out behind it. There was a second plume of dust, although the vehicle creating it was hidden by the first.

She hit the ground. She wasn't sure what to do. If she kept running, they'd probably see her. She had very few places to hide. But there were enough hollows and dips that, if she lay completely still, she might not be seen. She was still several hundred yards from the road. As she glanced back, she noted the two vehicles still had a ways to go. She bounced to her feet and darted cross-country away from the road again.

A clump of trees was up ahead and several bushes. She expected, if they had seen her, they'd figure that she'd race there for cover. But she had to do anything to keep hidden.

As she tripped into a creek bed, a dry hollow, she realized this was the perfect answer. She raked the dirt on top of her, and, with a couple rocks placed carefully around her face, she left her mouth and her injured head open between them, while covering up most of her. Her auburn hair, her pale skin, her freckles, even her beige T-shirt, they were all camouflage-worthy attire for her right now. Here she lay, her breathing shallow and heavy. She drank the last of her water, then lay still.

In the distance she could hear voices. She knew they had seen her.

"Where the hell did she go? Did you see her?"

"I saw her running about a hundred yards off," one of the men called. "Just keep walking. Keep walking."

She didn't dare breathe heavily. She lay as still as she could, frozen and waiting. She could hear footsteps in the distance, men still talking. God help her if one of them stepped on her.

"Search to the left. I saw her run that way."

"No, I don't think so," one of the men said. "There's no sign of her anywhere."

"If she was smart, she went for the trees," said yet a different man.

"Yeah, but, of course, that's the first place we would look for her," another man said.

Inside, she thought to herself, *Please, just keep walking. Just keep walking.* She knew, if they found her, it would be the end. This time, if they recaptured her, she'd have a much worse time escaping. Chances were they'd kill her.

"Okay, I'll head off to the trees. You guys keep scanning this area. Just keep walking. She couldn't have gone far."

"There's no place she can hide," one of the men said. "Look at this place. It's just dirt and rocks."

"She was wily enough to get free. She could have other tricks up her sleeve."

She could hear the men grumbling, but one man's voice got fainter. Probably heading for the copse of trees she had avoided. She knew they'd head there. Any sane person would. She figured she was the last person anybody would consider sane. She kept wishing for Ethan to hurry and find her.

And then the fear crept in again that he hadn't heard her message. That was so not what she needed to think now.

All of a sudden a couple heavy crunches of booted feet on rocks came close to her. From her left, one of the men called out, "Did you see anything?"

A man, almost upon her, called back, "Nah, there's nothing out here. Besides, if she is, she might as well stay out here and die. The desert will kill her in no time."

She winced. But he was right. Just because she'd escaped, didn't mean she was safe. The footsteps crossed in front of her as the man headed over to join the other men. She didn't dare move. And, no matter how curious she was, no way could she raise her head and remain unseen. All she could do was wait. Hopefully these guys would leave, and the right man would arrive.

But she didn't know how long that would take. She listened intently as the men's voices faded into the distance, and she heard a vehicle start up and take off again. She relaxed and thought that maybe, just maybe, she was free and clear.

The sun beat down, but, under the dirt, it was not too bad. She didn't dare get up, just in case it was a trick. Some of the men could have driven off and left the others to stand watch. She lay here in the heat of the sun and could feel her eyes growing weary.

Eventually she told herself, she'd nap to regain her

strength, just for a few minutes.

And she closed her eyes and fell asleep.

ETHAN FROZE AS he watched figures in the distance. Vehicles parked, armed men running around, but Ethan didn't see a woman. He let his gaze relax, becoming accustomed to the scene in front of him. He tried not to search for anything but rather have movement jar his awareness. He couldn't guarantee she was out here, but it was likely, given the location. He knew Levi was heading toward the main part of the camp. But Ethan saw no sign of Levi's vehicle, at least not from where he stood.

He was more concerned about the men, four that he could count, combing the acres of land between him and the next rise. He couldn't hear any sounds from this distance, but just their actions, their frantic movements, were enough to get reactions from the dogs. Bella and Sentry both stood, their backs bristled, a slight growling coming from deep in their throats. Ethan judged the distance between him and the gunmen to be a couple miles. Bella stood eagerly at attention, willing for whatever was coming.

The four gunmen continued in their search for Cinn, unaware of Ethan.

On that note, Ethan drank some of his water, then clipped it onto his belt, let Sentry choose the direction and started to run. Every step caused pain in his stump, but he ignored it. Cinn was going through something so much worse. Besides, Ethan had been working hard at training his injury.

The dogs were also injured but ran eagerly at his side.

Both leashed, both running level with him. He appreciated the training that had gone into their original care. He was just damn sorry they had ended up with somebody who had turned them into killers.

From where Ethan was, he didn't think he was visible, but again any movement on the horizon like this could catch the bad guys' attention. In the distance a movement caught his eyes. He turned to see a fox running away from him. He smiled and whispered, "Go, fella. We wish you well."

He turned his attention back to the men, seeing them split, two going one way, two heading toward the copse of tress. Most people in Cinn's position would head for the trees, hoping for a hiding place that would keep them safe. But, because it was the first place the men were likely to look, it was also, in this case, probably the worst thing she could do. But she wasn't a fool.

He kept running. It took a good three minutes to get his breathing even.

The terrain was rough, unsteady, his footsteps landing, occasionally rolling ever-so-slightly. It ate up his energy, this cross-country running. But it was necessary. He kept his eyes trained on the men ahead. They stopped, checked out the surrounding trees, and just then he heard a shout. The two closest to him turned and headed toward the others, all now heading for the copse of trees.

Ethan was still at least a mile out.

He kept up the pace, jogging steadily, needing a bit of good luck getting close without them noticing his approach. Just then the four men broke from the trees, stopped and stared. He hated to, but he stopped, minimizing the dust rising up around him. Crouched, he peered just over the rocks to see the men staring in his direction. He waited, the dogs at his side panting heavily, their gazes locked on the men in front of them. Good. They should know exactly who it was they were up against.

What he couldn't count on was the dogs' reactions when they reached the men. Would they see them as friend or foe? Would they listen to Ethan's commands or to the enemy's? Surely some of the men had befriended the dogs? But he would never get a better chance than here and now to see where their loyalties lay and to see if, in any way, he could redeem them. Bella had already proven herself to be trainable and loyal to him, but she hadn't been put to the real test yet. Sentry, on the other hand, he'd been trained to kill for these men, making him the bigger problem.

Still, Sentry had listened to Ethan over the intruder they had caught at Cinn's house. Would Sentry welcome a chance to go after these men? Or would he welcome them with yips and howls of joy and jump all over them? Ethan could only guess what would happen. Sentry certainly wasn't pulling back or resisting the run. Right now he wanted to tear ahead. Ethan just didn't know for sure why.

The men seemed to turn and look toward their vehicles; then they slowly marched back. Ethan stayed where he was, watching as, every once in a while a man turned his gaze, sweeping around, probably looking for Cinn, and maybe for Ethan. The question was, where was Cinn? And would the dogs pick up her scent? Was she hurt? Had she been shot again? Was she running for her life in a completely different area? Did she have any water?

It was too easy to lose somebody in this countryside. Without helicopters, without motion sensors, without any GPS tracking, finding her, especially in time if she was injured, would be hard. He didn't know if Levi had access to any satellite imagery, but, if they would be so lucky to have the police involved with similar technology, then maybe they would catch sight of her. Deeming it safe, he got up. Instead of running, he walked slowly, as the men were now all in their vehicles. Two of them drove ahead of the other two. Ethan didn't want to push his luck, waiting until they took the first corner.

Then he picked up the pace and ran toward the area where they'd been. Another vehicle drove toward him, but he couldn't tell who it was. He wished he had a better view. It would tell him if it was Levi meeting up with that group of gunmen, or if it would be more of the foes.

Taking a chance, he bent down, unclipped Bella, gave her a sniff of Cinn's jacket and told her to search. And Bella took off. Sentry tried to jump behind her, but he was still leashed. Ethan picked up the pace, running behind Bella, who was now flat-out racing across the countryside toward the road.

And there she stopped, milling around, and started to sniff. She wasn't a bloodhound. She was an attack dog. Ethan knew it was a slim chance that she'd pick up Cinn's scent, but all dogs seemed to have a sense for tracking that completely outshone anything humans could do.

He didn't know for certain about that with Sentry or Bella.

Finally reaching Bella, he gave her another sniff of the jacket, and she walked up and down the road, whining. "I know. Where could she be? Maybe she hitched a ride from someone?" He thought about that. There were just too many unknowns. As he looked to the left of the road, he realized nobody had gone that direction. He moved forward along the road to where the men had gotten out of their vehicles.

Bella and Sentry started to whine and howl, barking as they picked up the scent of the men who'd been here. He just didn't know what their reaction meant. He led the way to the trees, with Bella now racing ahead, following the men's trails.

"Sure, Bella. But do you want to see these guys, or is it because you can also smell Cinn's scent here?"

They were a good two minutes away from the trees. He walked slowly, his gaze roaming carefully across the sand and dirt.

She had to be here somewhere. His worst fear was that she'd collapsed, had been shot and was even now bleeding out into the dry ground.

Shots split the silence. He dashed into the tree line to make sure he and the dogs were out of the firing line. He peered through the trees to see what was going on. But there was just dust and chaos where the vehicles had met, face-to-face.

"Well, that answers that question," he muttered. "I'll take that as Levi met up with the enemy." Ethan bent down and gave Sentry a good scratch as he whined. "It'll be fine, buddy. I don't know about the fate of your previous owners, but you'll be fine. We need to focus on finding Cinn." He called Bella to him, and slowly, carefully, methodically went through the trees. He looked up in the branches, just in case she'd climbed up.

Deeming they were safe enough, he called out, "Cinn? Are you here? Call out if you're hurt. It's me, Ethan. I've got the dogs."

In a gentle voice he kept calling to her. But there was no answer. As he came to the end of the trees, he thought about going back down for another run, but so much land surrounded him. He couldn't spend too much time here.

He also couldn't be sure the men hadn't seen her, shot her and left her somewhere. He hadn't heard a sound, but, depending on how close they'd been, he might not have. If the wind had been moving up the hills, sweeping away from him, it could easily have been disguised. He glanced down at Sentry and held Cinn's jacket to his nose.

Sentry barked and strained at the leash. Bella came back over, milled around the two of them, sniffing the air and sniffing the jacket.

Ethan was taking a hell of a chance to let Sentry off his leash. He could disappear on Ethan. But he made a decision to give the dog some trust and to hope the dog would trust him back. Ethan reached down, unclipped the big harness off the dog's shoulders, and Sentry bolted cross-country into the area Ethan had not searched when coming in.

There was still a good mile of land out here that the dogs ran flat out into. But this time Bella was ever-so-slightly behind, and Sentry moved with intent. Ethan picked up his feet and raced forward. He didn't call out to the dogs. For all he knew, Sentry was headed back to the compound. But Ethan had to give Sentry a chance.

And suddenly Sentry came to a complete stop and barked.

CHAPTER 13

INN WOKE TO a horrific barking above her and a heavy weight on her chest. She shifted and then groaned. But she could hardly hear her thoughts. A dog barking outrageously stood on her torso, his head above her head. He terrified her. He was huge, looming over her, barking in her face. She wasn't sure, but she thought it was Sentry. But wasn't Sentry under Ethan's command? Or was Sentry now back under one of the assholes' control?

She knew she wouldn't have much time to make a decision. She could either bolt, and the dog would likely take her down, or she could lie here and hope the dogs didn't belong to the bad guys. Her heartbeat slammed against her chest, and the dog's drool dripped on her face. But she didn't move.

And then suddenly she heard someone call out, "Easy boy, easy boy." She strained her ears. Ethan?

"Bella! Come on, Bella."

Bella?

She smiled. "Ethan?" she called out weakly.

"Cinn?"

She managed to get her good hand under her and lifted her body. Dirt slid off her shoulders as she cried out, "Yes, it's me."

And suddenly there he was. He bent beside her, moving

Sentry off to the side, clipping him on a leash. His hand went to her head, brushing off the dirt. "Are you okay?"

She gave a broken laugh. "Yes. Bruised, my feet are killing me, but I'm alive. I buried myself in the dirt, so the assholes wouldn't find me. When the dogs arrived, I was terrified Sentry was working for the wrong team."

Ethan cleaned the dirt and rocks off of her. When he could, he reached down, grabbed her under the shoulders—careful of her injury—and helped her to a sitting position. She cried out when her bloody feet scraped along the ground. He lifted her feet, took one look at her soles and the gentlest wince whispered across his face.

"I couldn't find any shoes," she whispered, holding her feet up in pain. "The best I could do was these socks."

He gently removed the socks and held them up so she could see she had worn the soles right out of them.

She stared at them. "I really don't want to see what my feet look like."

"No," he said grimly. "You do not." He slowly lowered her feet so her calves rested sideways on his legs. "What about other injuries?"

She shook her head and shot a hand up to her head. "A headache—from those assholes knocking me out, I presume—and, of course, my shoulder," she admitted. "But everything else appears to be in good working order. I ran and walked as much as I could, following the road back out. But then I saw the vehicles coming after me, and I had to hide."

He glanced around at her hiding spot and smiled. "You did a great job."

"Not really," she said, motioning at the dirt. "Once I disturbed it and opened up a dark slash of dirt, the sun didn't have a chance to dry it out and turn the camouflage the same color as the rest of surroundings."

"But it was enough that you stayed hidden. They all headed to the trees."

"I know at least one was very close. I didn't dare look around to see where the others were," she said, her heart hitching at the reminder. "They were almost upon me. If they'd had the dogs, for sure they would have found me. And I couldn't keep my head completely buried because I had to breathe. But I was between the rocks, so it was deceptive. I was hoping they'd think some animal had disturbed this part of the dirt."

"It worked," Ethan said in an admiring tone. "You did good."

Just then she felt a wet nose against her face. She looked up to see Bella. "Hello, Bella," she murmured, gently scratching her thick neck. "Did you help find me?"

Bella nudged her, when her hand slowed down, and Cinn chuckled.

"Bella, lie down," Ethan ordered.

Bella lay down and dropped her head lower on Cinn's lap, so Cinn could scratch the rest of her.

She glanced over at Sentry and asked, "And him? Was he okay?"

"He found you," Ethan said proudly, reaching out to scratch the big male who again stared in the direction of the vehicles. "But we're still not out of danger here."

She looked in the direction Sentry was focused on. "What are you talking about?"

"Two vehicles came down and met up two of Levi's vehicles." He pointed to the other side of the trees. "I heard a lot of shooting, but I can't be sure who's left standing."

"And we're in the open," she cried out. She shook her head. "You should have left me here. I can't run anywhere right now."

He stood, looped her arms around his neck and picked her up. Moving at a steady pace, he walked back toward the trees.

"Not that I have anything against being carried," she joked, "but aren't the trees where they'll look for us?"

"Indeed it is," Ethan said. "But out here, like you said, we're sitting ducks. In the trees, we have a little more opportunity. Besides, the sun is very hot."

He walked steadily. She marveled at his strength. She wasn't a big woman, but, at the same time, it wasn't easy to hike while carrying someone else like this.

Finally they headed into the cooler shade of the trees. He found a large downed tree and sat her gently on the stump. "Now stay here, rest up against this tree. I would like very much to find out what's going on over there by the vehicles, but I don't want to leave you."

"No, please don't," she said. "Can't you stay here with me?"

"I'll leave Bella with you. I'll take Sentry and go over there." He pointed up ahead about forty feet. "I promise I'll stay in sight."

She nodded and let him go. She was too tired to protest. Her feet were killing her; her head pounded, and she wished he'd left her some water. She checked her bottle. There was just enough to wet the inside of her mouth. She hugged Bella and marveled at a dog who'd gone from being part of a killer pack to being part of a defending pack. And then she realized it really had nothing to do with choice. The dog was being swept along by the same nuances of society as Cinn herself was. There were only so many choices the dogs could make on their own, and they had to deal with the hand they were dealt. Bella was doing the best she could. At the moment she seemed happy to be with Cinn.

Cinn reached over and scratched her, pulling her ears gently, moving her hand down the side of the shepherd's face. "You're quite the beautiful girl, aren't you?"

Bella turned her head to look at her and then turned to follow Ethan's and Sentry's progress. Cinn could see the two sneaking out from behind one of the big trees, and she looked toward the vehicles. They might have been shooting at each other earlier, but she couldn't hear anything now.

And just then a cry rang out.

She almost fell off the log in surprise. She turned to see one of the men from the compound run in her direction. She swore gently, gripping Bella as she tried to get into a better position, but, as she tried to stand, her feet collapsed out from under her, and she fell onto the ground, leaning up against the log.

He was on her in an instant, his hand at her throat, closing around her windpipe, as he gave her a slap. "You little bitch," he roared. "We were looking for you."

Bella barked and launched herself forward.

"*Down*, Bella," her attacker ordered.

Bella subsided slightly, confused.

"I thought you were all shot," Cinn gasped when she could, her hand gripping his. His grip eased, and she choked and coughed.

"Not me," he said. "As soon as the shooting started, I snuck away and came back. I'm not up to face-to-face gunfire. A sneak attack is much more my style. Besides, I knew you had to be out here somewhere. But I checked here earlier, so I don't know how the hell you got here."

"I crawled," she lied. She could only hope Ethan and Sentry were well hidden from this asshat. "Besides, what do you want with me? I didn't do anything to you."

"I want that asshole boyfriend of yours," he said. "He's the one who came in with the cops, stole the dogs and blew up the entire operation at the compound."

She wanted to cheer Ethan's work but knew she would get a punch in the face for it. "Then why are you after me?"

"Because coming after you will lead to him." He sniggered. "That's the way it works. Use a piece of pretty bait, and the men just keep coming around."

She glared at him. "So you're the one who came after me? Broke into my house, terrorized my own dogs?"

"Me and Tom, yeah," he said. "Why? You didn't like that treatment? We were planning on coming back and showing you a good time. Imagine our surprise when you weren't there anymore."

She could hardly swallow for the bile rising up her throat. Just the thought of what these men would have done to her if she hadn't escaped …

He released her suddenly and said, "You didn't escape alone though, did you?"

He jumped behind the log, his hand going out to Bella, who stared at him, her lips curling. Cinn could understand Bella's confusion. He'd been aggressive but not deadly. And Bella was confused as to who to work with.

Cinn reached out and stroked Bella who whimpered and pushed her hand into her nose.

The man stared at Bella and said, "Jesus Christ, did you ruin her too?"

"Is she a killer?"

"No. She was like the other bitch, too soft. They said bitches make the best killers, but we always found they were too soft. Boris, on the other hand, now he's got the making of a killer."

"And what about this poor girl? What did you do to her?"

"We were training her to attack. She could run them down with the best of them," he said in a conversational voice. "But she held back from doing the final kill."

"It's not her nature," Cinn said, her fingers stroking and scratching Bella's neck.

The man sniggered and said, "It's every bitch's nature." He reached an arm around Cinn's neck and pulled her back, choking her.

Bella jump forward and barked.

The attacker glared at her. "Bella, *stand down.*"

Bella sat back down again and started to whimper. But her whimper turned to a growl, and then she barked again. Cinn understood. So much confusion, double masters, which way should Bella go?

"You could leave her alone and let her have a decent life," Cinn gasped. She reached up and clawed her attacker's arms. If nothing else, maybe the DNA in her nails would help catch this asshole if he did kill her.

He roared, snapped her head back against the tree and let her go. Then he smacked her on the side of the head and said, "You'll be sorry you did that."

Only Bella, it seemed, had enough evidence to make her decision. But he didn't give her a chance. He reached out and smacked her hard on the side of the head, knocking her to the ground. Cinn could hear Bella crying as she landed, but she bounced back up, growling and howling, this time darting in and darting back out again, avoiding his hands, snapping at his legs.

Cinn's head pounded, throbbing, as she lay here, desperate to move. The only thing she could do was roll. She stretched out and rolled onto the main path, hoping Ethan would see her.

But her attacker stood and lunged at her. Only a huge furry body jumped over Cinn and attacked first.

The man screamed in terror and pain.

Ethan's voice roared over the din at Sentry to stand down. Cinn rolled several more times until she saw Bella snapping at her intruder and Sentry looking for an opportunity to go in for the kill. A kill they couldn't let happen. She lay there trying desperately to stay out of the way.

Ethan stepped up and ordered, "Sentry, down."

Sentry's shoulders hunched, the ridge on his back high and long, his teeth bared, growling as he argued with Ethan's command.

But Ethan straightened, laid a hand on his shoulder and said, "Good dog. We've got him."

And suddenly the man broke and turned to run away.

Ethan took command and said, "Sentry, *attack.*"

Sentry took six huge jumps and threw himself eagerly in the air, landing on the man's back, face-planting him into the ground.

Ethan was on him and said, "Sentry, *stand down.*"

Sentry glared at him.

And then Ethan reached out a hand, completely ignoring the fact that Sentry was in full attack mode, stroked his head and said, "We've got him. Good dog. We don't kill anymore."

Sentry slowly calmed down. Ethan had him sit at the

man's left arm while he placed Bella at the man's right arm and slowly flipped the man to his back, holding him captive with his knees on his chest.

The man glared up at him. "What did you do to my fucking dogs?"

"Saved their lives, most likely," Ethan said calmly. "Why would you try to change these animals? They're perfect as they are."

"We needed animals that would kill. If they can't do the job, they don't need to be around. Same damn thing for employees. If you can't take that step, you're too damn weak to be with us."

"Yeah? And how many men have you killed because of it?"

The guy glared up at him and said, "Who the fuck knows. We've been doing this for a long time. It's not our problem a lot of assholes are out there."

Cinn managed to get herself into a sitting position and watched the men, now a good fifteen feet away. "That's not an answer," she snapped in a hard voice. She got on her hands and knees and slowly made her way closer.

Sentry, however, was between her and the attacker. He growled as she approached. She stopped and looked at Ethan.

Ethan looked over at Sentry. "Sentry, this is Cinn. You know her. She's a friend."

Sentry gave him a look as if to say, *What the hell?* As Cinn slowly, cautiously inched forward, Sentry subsided and let her approach.

She shook her head at Ethan. "Are you sure he's safe?"

Ethan said, his voice sure, calm, "There are times when having that killer instinct is helpful."

"See?" said the man pinned to the ground. "Like I said, killers are required."

Cinn settled on her butt and looked at Ethan, wondering if he considered killer dogs as a requirement, and then she remembered his military background and what he'd trained the dogs to do. She nodded. "Just remember. We're no longer at war," she said gently.

He stared at her, his gaze hard. Then he slowly seemed to calm, and his hardness eased. He pursed his lips. "You're right, at least not a war like I used to be in."

She nodded and reached out a hand to Sentry, who sniffed and then nudged his nose into her fingers so she could pet him. "Sentry, same for you. There'll always be assholes who we need protection from, but the least amount of force is the best."

At that, voices came from behind them. She turned to see Flynn. She lifted her arm as he dropped down beside her to give her a big hug. "I'm so glad to see you," she said.

Flynn called to Ethan, "Are you okay?"

And Ethan responded, "I'm good."

Flynn rose, lifted her up to stand on her feet so fast that she didn't get a chance to tell him that she couldn't. As soon as her feet hit the ground, she cried out. Pain shot up her legs, into her body and up to her head. It was just too much between the headache, the pain in her feet, her thirst and the shock. She crumpled into his arms.

ETHAN TURNED TO see Cinn as she collapsed in Flynn's arms. But already Levi and several other men raced to her side. The dogs growled and snarled at the new arrivals. It was all Ethan could do to hold them back and to calm them down. He got the leashes on both dogs and got them to sit under order.

Levi said, "It's hard to believe you've known them only a few days."

"Less than two days to be exact," Ethan said with a crooked grin. "We're still getting to know each other."

Levi's eyebrows rose. "I wasn't so sure when we first arrived. Thought we might have a problem on our hands." He motioned toward Sentry. "But it looks like things are under control."

"They are," Ethan said, "but they're still new to being on the good side." He motioned to the man on the ground. "These assholes were training the dogs to kill."

"And did they?"

Ethan didn't really want to admit it. He shrugged and said, "Depends if you can believe what this guy says. But it's possible."

Levi nodded. "We both know dogs in the military that had to do the same thing."

Ethan felt something inside him relax at that because Levi knew. Just like Ethan knew. He nodded his head, his emotions stronger, feeling on firmer ground. "Yes. It's all about discerning when it's necessary."

"Exactly."

Levi turned and frowned at Cinn, held closely in Flynn's arms. He walked over as Ethan approached with the dogs at his side.

Ethan explained, "Her feet have run down to nothing. When Flynn stood her up, it was too much."

Flynn turned so Levi could see the soles of her feet.

Levi winced. "That's just plain hamburger stuck to the

end of her bones." He motioned toward the vehicles. "Let's get her to the hospital, where we can get her treated. Where'd you leave your vehicle?"

Ethan pointed back where he'd come from. "About three miles that direction."

Levi said, "If you want to ride in the back of the truck with the dogs, you're welcome."

Ethan grinned. "That's the perfect place for the three of us."

Together the large crew walked back out of the trees, leading Cinn's attacker to the vehicles.

"We heard gunshots," Ethan said, studying Levi. "How bad is the damage?"

"On our side, none," Levi said cheerfully. "On the other side, three dead."

Cinn's attacker roared and stopped walking to look at them. "What?"

Levi nodded. "If you'd stayed, you would be dead too. Maybe it's too bad you didn't."

But that was enough said. The man fell silent as he contemplated the fate of his friends.

Back at the truck, Ethan got the dogs into the bed, and he sat down against the cab with them. He continuously worked on their commands, letting them know they were still in working mode. Within five minutes they were at the spot where he'd parked his truck, and he transferred the dogs.

Then he got into the driver's side. He needed to take the dogs back home first. He would have to deal with the police and check on Cinn at the hospital.

So first things first, he started up the engine and headed home. He didn't know if it was all over for sure, but he could damn well hope so. He figured this mess was, but there would always be a new one out there to deal with. Still, with the dogs at his side, he wasn't against being part of the fight.

In his driveway, his phone rang. He hopped out of his truck, pulled out his phone and answered it. It was Sergeant Mendelsson.

"I hear you had fun this morning."

"I'm not sure that's what we'd call it," he said, "but the dogs found Cinn, and she's relatively unhurt, so that's what counts."

"How do you think you'll do with their training?"

Ethan wondered if he'd be plagued with those questions from now on, but, in a steady voice, he explained how well both Bella and Sentry had done, how they both needed some training, to work on *fetch, find*, search-and-rescue work, but that Sentry had been called off from taking down and killing the attacker.

"Is this something you want to stick around and work on?" the sergeant asked curiously.

"I'd like to think so," Ethan said. Gunner has asked me to train some dogs for him."

"Well, if he thinks you can do it, then that's a pretty decent referral right there. I spoke with Levi, and he backs up your story. Nice to know you had control of the animals at the scene too."

"I did. Obviously the relationship between the three of us is still young, but it's there. And Bart and Sally are great additions too."

"Good. So are you interested in doing contract work? Because, if you are, get those dogs up and running, then give me a call."

Ethan grinned and gave Bella a good stroke. She dropped her nose to shove it into his face. "I think we could do something like that. I'll have four able-bodied dogs here pretty soon."

"Then it sounds like you might need another handler."

Ethan shrugged. "If somebody else with the skills comes my way … In the meantime, I can handle four myself."

"Good, we need someone like you," he said, "But it's not just us. Consider the airport, consider private security. I think you've got yourself quite a business right here."

After the sergeant hung up, Ethan pocketed his phone, reached for the tailgate, let the dogs out, led them around to the back, where Bart happily greeted them all. Ethan gave them all food and water and walked inside. He kneeled beside Sally and asked, "How are you doing, girl?"

And his heart smiled as she rolled over and struggled to her feet. He led her a little way outside, so she'd go to the bathroom. She walked over to him afterward and nudged his hand gently. He bent down into a squatting position and spent a few moments just loving her.

"You know what? Maybe that is a good idea. Start with rescuing dogs, then retraining. We could train in many different specialties—drug-sniffing, bomb-smelling, guard dogs. Who knows what else we could do?" he murmured into her fur. "Maybe it's a new beginning for all of us."

Sally barked gently, and the other three dogs ran over. Ethan chuckled. She barked again, nudging at his coat pocket. And he laughed because, of course, he had dog treats in his pocket. Every decent dog trainer had treats. He reached into his pocket and pulled out four and gave them each one. Maybe he was finally home. Just like for the dogs, something was here for all of them.

Now all they had to do was convince Cinn that she belonged with them too.

CHAPTER 14

C INN WOKE UP, lying on the backseat of a twin-cab truck driving at a steady pace. She listened to the conversation going on around her. She couldn't be too badly hurt because nobody was crying over her. But her feet sure hurt.

As she struggled to sit up, Flynn, who was sitting beside her, put a hand on her good arm, telling her to lie back down. She smiled up at him. "Where's Ethan?"

"He's taking the dogs home. I'm sure he'll be at the hospital soon."

She winced at the term *hospital*. "My feet?"

"I suspect so," Flynn said with a bright cheerful smile. "At least if that's what you call them. Levi said they look like hamburger on sticks."

She groaned. "Please tell me that they're not that bad. I'll be bedridden for weeks."

"They're that bad," Levi said from the driver's seat.

Soon the big hospital building rose up in front of them.

Levi parked in front, and Flynn got out. She struggled to sit up and made her way to the edge of the seat. She was not looking forward to getting down. As a matter of fact, just the thought sent waves of nausea to her stomach.

As she tried to stand, Levi arrived at Flynn's side. "No, you don't," he said. "That's what this is for."

They had a wheelchair. Levi reached up, and she put her

good arm around his neck. He scooped her off the seat and plunked her gently onto the chair. Then they did something to the footrests so her legs stuck out straight.

She said, "I don't even know what they'll do for them. They're so dirty." She looked down at herself. "I mean, I was buried in the dirt, so I guess all of me is a huge mess."

"And for that reason alone," a smiling nurse said, greeting them at the doorway, "we may just take you in the wheelchair into a special shower and see what we find underneath all that dirt." The large portly woman smiled down at Cinn. "I hear you've had a rough morning."

"Tough night and a rough morning," Cinn said with a smile. "But this is a much better-looking afternoon."

At that the woman laughed, got behind the wheelchair and pushed Cinn forward. "We'll get some information from you, but we really won't see anything until we get you cleaned up."

"Are you serious about a shower?"

"Can you tell us if you've got any other injuries?"

"My head was bashed in." Cinn thought about it and said, "I don't know how bad they are, but there's some scrapes and bruises. And, of course, a previously treated gunshot wound to my shoulder."

"In that case, yes, just to be sure. You were kidnapped, and you've got a head injury. If the doctor okays it, I think we'll get you cleaned up first, get those feet soaking, and we'll see what else might need to be done."

And that's what they did. It took a good thirty-five minutes though before she was okayed, and the nurse took her into a completely different area of the hospital, pushed open a door to let her into a series of bathrooms with a large wheel-in shower. With the nurse's help, she was undressed and, still in the wheelchair, put into the shower.

There, the nurse helped her shampoo until they could check the head wound. "I feel something running down my face," Cinn said. "Please tell me it's shampoo." She felt so much better just being clean.

"No, it's not," the nurse said. "That's blood from the head wound."

"I was hoping it wasn't that bad."

"They tend to bleed a lot. A couple stitches should put that one to rights, but the cleaner we can get it and everything else, the better it'll be. Otherwise we'll have to cut away a bit of your hair there."

Gently avoiding the head wound as much as she could, she scrubbed down, loving the water streaming down her body. As the nurse noted, several of Cinn's ribs were pretty bruised, but nothing was as bad as her feet.

When she was all cleaned up, she sat with her feet out, letting the water run over them. "I don't think this is getting the soles."

"No," the nurse said. "We'll have to soak them in hot soapy water with antiseptic. Then the doctor can take care of your head."

She was soon on a bed, wearing a hospital gown with a robe over it, sitting up with her feet in a big bucket of warm soapy water with antiseptic. The doctor sat on a stool, poking and prodding at her hairline. Needles went in for numbing, then sutures closed her scalp wound.

Finally the doctor said, "Now let me check the rest of you, see what has happened. The ribs don't appear to be broken. You're banged up. The shoulder wound, ... well, it's a little worse but will hold. We can get the feet back in good shape, so you'll be just fine."

She smiled up at him, the fatigue of the day hitting her hard. "Honestly, if I could sleep for a few hours, I think I'd feel a ton better."

"And sleep is what you need. But those feet have to be cleaned up first."

She nodded. "How bad do they look?"

He lifted one up and took a look and then sighed. "Let's just say, you won't like the next hour or so."

She sat bolt upright and said, "Why not?"

"Because soaking has taken off a lot of the dirt, but rocks are embedded in the cuts, and we have to clean out lots of little bits and pieces. I'll put some numbing gel on them, and I'll give you a shot for the pain."

By the time they were done, she was in agony. The tears had flowed, and she lay on her belly, her feet elevated. The nurse finally put a soothing ointment over Cinn's soles. Just her touch made Cinn cry again.

The nurse finally said, "There, you're done."

Her muscles relaxed. She hadn't realized how tense she'd been. She lifted her head and gave the nurse a watery smile. "Thank God for that."

The nurse, obviously distressed at the pain she had put Cinn through, nodded. "It is one of the worst jobs I have to do. I'm so sorry."

Cinn shook her head. "It's not your fault. Thank you for cleaning them up."

As the nurse cleaned up the mess from the medications and the bandaging, she said, "Now you just lie there and rest. Close your eyes. When you wake up, if you're in pain, we'll give you some more medication."

On that note, the nurse walked out. Cinn lay here, wondering what had happened to Flynn and Levi. But then she didn't care because sleep dragged her under, and honestly, it was the only place she wanted to go.

ETHAN WALKED INTO the hospital and headed to the reception area. "Cinnamon Michelson was brought in this morning with damaged feet. If she's still here, may I see her?"

The receptionist nodded. "She was brought in this morning. She's still in emergency, I believe."

Frowning, Ethan made his way over to emergency and was stopped by an orderly. He explained who he was and who he was looking for.

The orderly held up a hand and said, "Now, that little girl needs sleep. Let me go take a look." He turned and peered through a curtain and studied what was probably Cinn on the bed, then he came back. "She's still sleeping."

Ethan nodded. "May I sit beside her then?"

The orderly looked at him and frowned. "Family?"

"No," Ethan admitted. "But maybe soon."

At that, the orderly chuckled. "In that case, you go right in, but don't wake her. Understand?"

Ethan nodded and stepped behind the curtain. One chair was at Cinn's bedside. He pulled it up closer and sat down but not before he took a solid look at her feet. He sucked in his breath at the lacerations and the bloody pulpy look to them. Cleaning the wounds had to have been the worst. Though they would heal, it would take time.

From his chair he reached out, sliding his fingers into hers. He sat here and waited for her to stir.

It was another ten to fifteen minutes before she lifted her eyelids and smiled. "Ethan. How's Sentry? Bella?" she asked, worry tinting her voice. "And Bart? Sally?"

He leaned over, kissed her cheek and said, "Sentry is fine. So are the others. How are you?"

"I'll be looking for a houseboy to keep me off my feet for the next week or two," she said with a chuckle and winced. "Don't think I'll be doing any walking, much less running, anytime soon."

"How's the shoulder?"

"They checked it and said it was healing," she said. "But I'm not sure the doctor wants to see me ever again."

Just then the curtain was pulled back, and the doctor stepped into the room. "I'd love to see you again but without being shot or kidnapped, okay?" He checked her feet. "You can go home, *but* you can't be alone. You're not allowed to stand on these feet at all."

She looked at him. "I have to go to the bathroom on my own."

"No, you don't," he said. "We are talking a wheelchair and lots of padding around these feet. You'll have to shift and shuffle your butt from one to the other. But no walking. You can stand for a short time, but you'll find you don't want to stand at all. If you have no one, we will see about home care visits."

She sank back into the bed. "You know I live alone, right?"

"Not for the next week or two you don't," the doctor said. "I'll write a prescription for the pain meds." He disappeared through the curtain.

She groaned. "I wonder if I can get one of my girlfriends to move in."

"Not an issue," Ethan said. "I'm not a girlfriend, and hardly a houseboy, but maybe you'll classify me as a boyfriend. I'm moving in and looking after you."

She propped herself up on her good elbow. "You don't have to do this because you feel guilty, you know?"

"How about I do this because I want to?" he said, leaning across and kissing her on the tip of her nose. "And I do feel guilty. I was supposed to look after you. And, well, I was dealing with one intruder, while the second guy came in and stole you away. Of course I feel guilty."

She frowned.

He lifted a finger, placing it against her lips. "I'm not arguing with you about it. Bottom line is, you need care, and I can give you care."

"I really don't want to think about you carrying me to the bathroom," she announced in dismay.

"You may not have a choice," he said. "Would you rather it be a stranger?"

She wrinkled up her face and shook her head.

"Good, then no arguments. I'll take care of the paperwork. Then we'll get you moved back home again."

"What about the dogs?"

He turned to look at her. "I was thinking about that. How do you feel about the five of us moving in?"

She laughed. "You know what the neighbors will say?"

"No, I don't know what they'll say, and I don't care what they'll say." He folded his arms over his chest. "Do you?"

She thought about it for a moment and shook her head. "No, I don't. But this isn't an invitation to come into my bed. You know that, right?"

"That invitation has been there right from the beginning, whether you're aware of it or not," he said, leaving her gasping in surprise. "And, when you're feeling better, I'll take you up on it, though not for the next few days. Right now you need care, and I'm the one who'll be there, ready to give you that care." He turned and walked out. He had to because he was laughing so hard.

He stopped, pushed aside the curtain and saw her struggling to sit up. He leaned in, placed a gentle hand on either side of her head and kissed her. When he tried to pull back, he found he couldn't. Instead he pulled her closer into his arms and deepened the kiss, letting her know with absolutely no doubt the direction they were headed. When he finally lifted his head and looked down at her face, he said, "See? Invitation all the way."

He dropped a kiss on her nose, turned and walked out.

CHAPTER 15

A FTER FIVE DAYS at home, she was angrier, more frustrated and pissed off than she could imagine. Ethan wouldn't leave her alone. He'd disappear for five minutes, and he'd be back before she had a chance to move. Like now. She'd asked him for a glass of water, so she could go to the bathroom—alone—but he was already standing in front of her, holding her water. She sat on the edge of her bed and glared at him.

He shook his head, crossed his arms over his chest and said, "You can try standing tomorrow. That's what the doctor said." And with that he spun on his heels and left.

"He didn't say I couldn't try earlier," she cried out.

"Yes, he did. He said to stay off your feet."

"That means stay off my feet *most* of the time," she said in exasperation. "Nobody in their right mind would expect me to stay off my feet all the time."

He poked his head around the corner of the doorway. "Absolutely not. The minute you put more pressure on those feet, you'll damage the blood vessels, and you'll slow the healing process. Now get your butt back down and get your feet up."

She flung her head back on the bed and put her feet back up on the stack of pillows he had placed there for her. It was really humiliating. The only way she managed to get any privacy was by crawling across the floor, getting into the bathroom on her own, using the bathtub for support in order to get to the toilet. She hadn't had a bath or shower in five days, *five days*, and she was dying for one. He had offered but also said he'd carry her there and help her get stripped down. She wasn't having anything to do with that.

But, if she made it to the bathroom, maybe she could make it into the bathtub on her own. Because one thing she did need was a damn good wash. In order to make that happen and to not get in deep trouble, she had to assure herself and him that she could do it without her feet touching the floor.

With a grin, she rolled over to lie on her belly and slid off the edge of the bed to land on her knees. She may have landed a little too heavily because instantly he was back inside her bedroom, checking up on her. She glared at him from her hands-and-knees position and said, "I'll have a bath whether you like it or not." She crawled over to the bathroom, her feet up in the air.

"You could at least ask me to run the water for you," he said, stepping ahead of her. "You don't have to be so stubborn all the time."

He walked into the bathroom, and the dogs followed. At the moment, they had Bella and Sally with them. Plus her two dogs. She was overwhelmed in K9s who all thought it was a great game having her at their level. She laughed and spent a few moments cuddling each one as she heard the water pouring in the bathtub.

She didn't know why she was being so feisty, but it was just impossible to be around him. She didn't even know what the issue was, but she hated feeling like an invalid. And she hated being catered to. He did it with such a happy-go-lucky smiling expression that she wanted to hit him half the time.

When he came back out, she said, "You can't be so nice all the time."

At that comment he squatted in front of her. "Why? You want me to be mean and nasty?"

She shrugged irritably. "You're pissing me off."

"I noticed," he said with a smirk.

She glared at him.

"There's an easy answer to it."

She frowned. "What's that?" she asked suspiciously.

"You're not ready for it yet."

And that did it again. She crawled past, ignoring him. She hadn't really been inviting him to share her bed. Well, maybe she had been, but she would put it down to the pain and the medications. He was too irritating for her to want to spend any more time with.

But inside she knew she was lying to herself. She just didn't want to feel incapable of living the life she wanted to live. It was a temporary situation, and she should stop acting like a spoiled brat and start feeling grateful. It was one thing to know that, but it was another thing to do it.

She maneuvered her way into the bathroom, shooing the dogs out as she tried to work her way past them. She shut the door, turned around and locked it. Feeling immeasurably happier, she twisted around so she sat on the floor and quickly shimmied out of her pajama bottoms. Carefully she pulled the socks off her feet, wincing at the tenderness of them, and stripped off the rest of her clothing.

Ethan knocked on the door and said, "You've got an hour. That's it."

"And then what?" she called out.

"I'm coming in to help because I'll assume you can't get out on your own," he said with a light warning.

She growled and then laughed because it was a fair time frame. It took a little more effort to maneuver herself up to rest on the bathtub edge so she could carefully maneuver herself over and into the water. Awkwardly she splashed down on her butt, her feet hanging off the side of the tub, water coming up and over the sides of the bathtub to the floor on the other side.

It felt so damn good to get into the water, she lay here with her feet dangling for a long moment, just letting her head sink into the gently rocking water.

After a few minutes she sat up and slowly lowered her feet into the water. She knew this would be the real test. Her feet had been cleaned and were definitely healing, but they were still sore and tender. She moaned in delight when they were finally submerged. She should have done this way earlier.

She reached for the shampoo and proceeded to scrub her scalp and then, with soap, scrubbed the rest of her. She tried to examine the soles of her feet, but it was hard to see in this lighting. They looked so much better. There were scabs and definitely tight pink tissue, signs of healing, but they were still puffy.

She knew that standing on them would hurt like crazy. Another couple days and they should be better. The doctor told her it would take about a week, and then she needed to walk with multiple socks on in order to give her feet the cushion they would need. And she'd also find it hard to stay on them for very long. That was all good. She was totally okay to follow *those* doctor's orders. So why was she being so bitchy?

Sure, being an invalid was part of it, but it was also having Ethan around all the time. They were dancing around in this newbie relationship of theirs, but she was in no position to move it forward. She wasn't even sure how to move it forward.

He'd taken on the role of a comfortable brother, almost. And that was very unsexy, going against where she thought they were heading. He was a really good man, she admitted. Too good a man maybe, she thought with a laugh.

But that wasn't true. He never lost his temper, but she could see the darkness in him. The pain. He'd been through some tough times. When he was asleep, she heard him cry out. She never asked him about PTSD, but she was sure that kept him up in the night. He had his secrets, and she had hers, although hers were pretty minor. They were getting to know each other. And she'd only found more to like.

Still, he was doing everything he could to help her get through this, and she appreciated it.

By the time she was done, had the water drained and sat on the bathtub's edge again, she wished she'd had a few more days of recovery time under her belt. She was wrapped up in a towel, but it would be hard to get back to the bed. There was no rush; she still had time before Ethan took over. She was sure he'd heard her get out anyway.

She pulled on pajamas again, and, now fully dressed, a towel wrapped around her head, she pulled another towel down and crawled on top of it back to the bed. It helped preserve her knees a bit.

Before she could get back in the bed, strong hands reached down, picked her up around the waist, and lifted her onto the bed. She let out a cry, not hearing him come up behind her. "You scared me," she scolded.

"Well, if you'd let me know that you could use a hand, then you wouldn't have been surprised," he said, his exasperation coming through his voice.

She flipped around and sat down on the bed, looking up at him. "I'm sorry. I'm being difficult, and I don't mean to be."

His gaze warmed. He sat on the bed beside her and said, "Have you figured out why you are?"

She waved a hand off to the side. "I don't like being an invalid. I don't like being treated like a child or being in a position of needing so much help," she said with a half smirk. "Particularly from you."

His eyebrows shot up. "What's wrong with me?"

She realized he'd taken it as an insult. She tried to get the words out correctly, but every time she tried to formulate her thoughts, she couldn't say them. Finally she raised her hands in frustration and said, "I don't want you to see me as helpless."

He stared at her for a long moment, stroked her cheek and said, "What I see is a valiant, strong woman who survived a terrible ordeal. The ordeal was brought on by me. And I'm doing everything I can to help you get back on your feet."

"I knew it," she cried out. "You feel sorry for me. You feel guilty."

"It's because of me that you're hurt. But, no, I don't feel sorry for you. I'm saddened this happened. But obviously you'll get better, and it's not a permanent injury. So I'm just helping you where I can." He stared at her for a long moment, then tapped the tip of her nose. "Is something else going on here?"

She snapped her lips closed and glared at him.

He nodded. "I'm not sure what's going on. Yet I understand a lot of it," he admitted, "because nobody likes to be treated or thought of as helpless. We all want to be independent."

She sighed and held out her hand. He covered hers with his and squeezed her fingers gently. "What are we doing here?" she asked softly.

His gaze locked on hers, and he smiled a slow, gentle smile that made her heart weep with emotion. "What is it you want to see us do here?"

She shook her head. "Oh, no you don't. You're not answering a question with a question."

He chuckled. "I'd like to get to know you better," he said. "I'd like to see where this goes."

"Are you planning on moving back to your own house?" she asked with a laugh. "Or are you planning on moving in here?"

He tilted his head to the side, his gaze twinkling. "Is the latter an option?"

She chuckled. "I hadn't planned on a house guest. But it is a big house."

"I have a place in town, as you know, but you have acres here for training exercises, plus the dog runs. But I think we're getting ahead of ourselves."

"How long do you think you need to be here looking after me?"

"You go back to the doctor in two days. If he says you can start walking around a little bit, then we'll see how it goes. Plan on maybe four days, and then I'll move back out again," he promised.

She smiled. "That sounds fair. And thank you very much for looking after me."

He shook his head. "Don't say that. I'm happy to do this. You know that." He leaned forward and kissed her gently.

She wrapped her arms around his neck and tugged him closer, turning a light kiss into a real kiss. When he straightened and pulled away, his gaze was searching, and she smiled up at him. "Why do you really think I've been snappy?"

He narrowed his gaze.

She nodded. "It wasn't an invitation," she said, referencing what he had said before, then admitted, "but in a way it was."

He smiled, then kissed her on the tip of her nose. "I know."

She pulled back slightly, changed the angle of their position and kissed him. "I guess we're not quite ready for this stage," she said, "but it would be nice if we were."

His gaze darkened. When he gave her a kiss this time, it took her to the depths of a passion she hadn't expected to see so fast. It left her gasping and surprised, wanting so much more.

When he straightened, she collapsed on the bed, just staring at him.

He grinned. "It depends on you," he said. "I've already expressed my interest."

"Oh, no you haven't," she said in astonishment. "At least not in so many words."

"I'm living in your house, looking after you," he said. "How is that not telling you that I care about you?"

She frowned. "That's just your guilt talking."

He gently picked her up, twisted her so she sat in his lap, tilted her head back and kissed her again. When he lifted his head this time, he said, "Guilt?" And he lowered his head again.

When he finally lifted his head the next time, she had all but melted in his arms. "This is not guilt," he whispered against her lips, his hand brushing her hair back once, then twice. "It's concern. It's caring. It's wanting to make sure somebody I want to spend time with is doing okay. Yes, a smidgen of guilt is in there, but it's more about wanting to spend time with you, making sure you are okay."

She nodded with a smile and said, "But that's not the same thing as wanting to take another step in a relationship. If we're just friends, then let's just stay friends."

He chuckled. "Was that kiss like a kiss between friends?"

"I have no clue," she said, confused herself at this point. She wished he'd just kiss her again and stop the talking.

As he went to put her back on the bed, she shook her head, slung her arm around his neck, grabbed hold and tugged him toward her. "My turn."

This time she kissed him. She hadn't realized how much she'd bottled up inside. This was what she wanted. It was what she'd wanted days ago, maybe longer. She didn't normally accelerate relationships, but no doubt they had something they needed to work through. She didn't know that bed was the best way to do it, but it sure would take some of the stress off. And what she wanted was a whole lot more than stress relief. She wanted to know they had something here they could build on ...

He pulled back and looked at her. "It's too soon," he said, his voice thick.

"Why? What do my feet have to do with this?"

"Your shoulder ..."

She glanced at her shoulder. "Well, your kisses are so distracting, I didn't even notice," she admitted. "I don't think it will be a problem."

His breathing came out in raspy breaths, and she could feel his heart pounding against her chest—both reassured her. She smiled up at him and whispered, "Unless you don't want to …"

He lowered his head and crushed his lips against hers. She shifted as the pain shot through her shoulder, but the passion quickly caught her and dragged her back under the surface. And her shoulder ceased to exist. In fact, when she roused from his drugging kisses, she found herself completely nude, lying on the cool sheets, and somehow he was there beside her, almost stripped down. "Wow. You made that happen fast."

He placed a finger against her lips and then replaced it with his own, and she was caught up in the maelstrom of his passion igniting hers and taking her back under until she no longer knew where she started and where he took over. It was an experience like none other. It was more emotion than she was used to. It was less about bodies and more about feelings.

Time flew as they tried to learn everything they could about each other. Conversation came in bits and pieces as they explored and questioned. She found the wounds on his chest, the scars on his back, the damage to his thigh, his stump. He was so adept with his prosthetic that she often forgot he was missing a leg. Every point she reached down to kiss and caress, and then asked him about them.

He finally pulled her up to rest on top of his chest and whispered, "Maybe a little less conversation?"

She smiled, shifted on his chest, drew her knees up to either side of him, and stretched up, resting against his erection. "We can always talk later," she said in a teasing murmur.

"We can also do this again later," he said. "At least I hope we can." He ran his hands over the top of her thighs to her hips, where he held her tight against him and started to shift.

She covered his hands with her own, and, using his hands for strength, rose and fell as she started to ride. She couldn't imagine where any of this had come from. Normally sex was a fast coupling, but this was learning who he was inside, at a level she'd never experienced before. It was special. It was slow. Until it wasn't slow anymore, and suddenly she couldn't talk any longer.

She threw her head back and let the emotions and the passion take over. She moved as her body wanted to move, letting her emotions and her feelings take charge. When he gripped her hips with his hands and picked up the pace, driving into her faster and faster, she matched him thrust for thrust.

Soon her body started to splinter apart; she arched, crying out as her world exploded.

He shifted until she was underneath him, and he drove once, twice, three times, and finally his own orgasm rolled over him. He collapsed beside her and held her close.

It was a long moment later when she whispered, "I've never experienced anything like that."

"What, an orgasm?" he teased.

"No," she said, shifting onto her arm. "Making love where it was okay to talk, where it was okay to ask questions, where it was okay to show emotion. Where it wasn't just following a road map from point A to point B, so you could get there the fastest route." She reached out to stroke a scar on his chest. "That it was okay to take time to explore and to understand, to really learn who you are."

He pulled her head down, so he could kiss her thoroughly. And when he let her go, she sagged against his chest.

"That's very addictive."

"I'm glad to hear it," he said with a soft chuckle. "Maybe we can do this again."

"I sure hope so," she said, a yawn sneaking out of her mouth. "I'm really not into short-term relationships, so I hope you're in for a long one."

He stroked the hair off her forehead and whispered, "Absolutely. That's what I figured we were here for, ... for a long time, not just a good time."

"How about both?" she whispered and slowly drifted off to sleep.

HE HELD HER close as she slept, until his phone rang. He shifted her to the side and sat up grabbing his pants. Pulling his phone from his jeans pocket, he answered it. "Jimbo, what's up?"

"Been hearing about you and some K9 dogs. As you know I've been working at the US War Dog Association. I'm not sure if you're setting up training or maybe a rescue, but I've got a female here. Her front leg was damaged from a mine explosion. She's being shipped stateside, but her foster family deal fell through because she has special needs."

They both went silent. Ethan could hear the rustling of papers.

"You might even know this one. Her name is Jessie, for Jezebel."

Ethan caught his breath in the back of his throat. "I saw

her as a puppy."

"Yeah, she's not quite four now. But she won't be working in the field anymore."

Ethan frowned, thinking about the beautiful shepherd she'd been. Small, but she was incredibly fast and very intelligent. "You mean, because she's missing a leg?"

"Yeah, and she's lost her nerve," Jimbo said. "At least that's what the notes here say."

"I'll take her," Ethan said immediately. "I have no clue what kind of business I'll end up with here, but it seems like rescuing working dogs is part of it."

He slowly put his phone on the night table beside him and lay back down. As soon as he was stretched out, Cinn curled up at his side.

"Why do I think this will involve way more dogs than the current four—make that five—now?"

"Because it definitely will." He hugged her close and whispered, "We'll need a bigger place."

She propped up so she could cross her arms on his chest and look down at him. "*We?*"

He reached up, flicked her nose with a smile and whispered, "*We.* You, me and all the dogs we could possibly handle."

Tears came to her eyes. She leaned down, brushed a kiss across his chest and whispered, "I'm in."

"I'm in too," he whispered back.

And they kissed, a gentle kiss, full of promise, full of tomorrows and, with any luck, full of K9s they had yet to meet.

CHAPTER 16

WITH CINN SLEEPING gently beside him, Ethan sent a text, updating Badger. Just then his phone rang. He shifted out of bed and hopped out into the hallway, trying not to wake up Cinn.

"Hey, glad to hear you're doing okay. Sounds like it was bit rough though," Badger said. "Good news on K9:01. Are you keeping the name Sentry?"

"I haven't given you all the details yet," he said, laughing. "And yes, I've gone back to calling him Sentry. He's been called Boris for the last while, so it might be hard on him for a bit."

"Maybe, but he'll adapt. And now you've got what, four dogs?"

"Yes, although a fifth is on the way. I've got Sentry and the dogs that came with him and Jezebel is being shipped from the War Dog Association. They are all a mix of both breeds and skills. But still, I can work with them all."

"That should keep your hands full."

Ethan winced, knowing Badger was referring to the other dogs he had said he would find. "In a way, yes," he said. He added more slowly, "And I'm sorry, but I'm not sure I'll go after any of the other dogs."

"Doesn't sound like it," Badger said with a laugh. "And that's all good. We didn't expect that. If it had worked out that way, great, but, considering you just inherited four, five dogs, … and maybe a new girlfriend, … sounds like you are exactly where you belong." There was a pause on the line, then Badger added thoughtfully, "But it would help us if you had any idea who might be interested."

"Talk to Pierce Carlton. Last I heard, he was helping Jager out on a security issue, I think. Pierce has a lot of K9 experience." Ethan paused. "We haven't spoken much about it, but I know he spent five years heavily involved in the DOD's Military Working Dog Breeding Program at Lackland Air Force Base in San Antonio. He was injured, and, while in the hospital, his wife divorced him and somehow took damn near everything he owned. So he's at loose ends, trying to find a new direction. This might not be it, but it could be a step in the right direction for him."

"If you think he'd have any interest in tracking down a dog, that would be huge," Badger said. "I'll call him and see what he says. We've got eleven more dogs to find. And now, buoyed by the success of finding this first one, it would be nice to give positive reports on the others."

"You'll let the commander know about Sentry?"

"Absolutely," Badger said. "Stay in touch, you hear?"

Ethan grinned. "Will do."

EPILOGUE

P IERCE CARLTON TOOK the next exit onto Highway 14, heading to Fort Collins. He wondered what he'd gotten himself into by agreeing to look for Salem, a black female shepherd who might or might not be missing. He'd been planning to come back to Colorado anyway; at least that was what he told himself. In truth he should have come back for a visit a long time ago. This was just a valid reason to do so.

In theory, handlers and dogs weren't supposed to get too attached. He'd snorted the first time he'd heard that because how could one not?

Still, this dog had been last seen in the community of Arrowhead outside of Fort Collins. Hence his stop here. If he remembered right, a small café was along this main boulevard that had absolutely the best apple pie you could buy. He pulled up to the café called Marge's and walked in. If ever a name could make you think of apple pie, it was a name like that. He hopped on in and stopped and smiled. Right in front of him was a large glass case with lots of what looked to be homemade baked desserts.

His stomach growled.

A portly woman walked toward him. "Well, that's a sound I like to hear."

He looked at her in surprise. "Please don't tell me that you can hear my stomach from all the way over there," he joked.

She smiled and nodded. "My ears are trained for that. Come on in and take a seat. We'll get some food in that belly."

But he didn't want to leave the glass case in front of him. "What's the deal with all these treats?"

"Well, they're for sale," she said. "Is that what you mean?"

"Are they fresh-baked? Home-baked? Or brought in from a city somewhere?"

"I bake all my own pies here," she said proudly. "I'm Aunt Marge." She held out a big beefy arm and a rotund muscly hand.

He gave it a good shake and knew she did the baking herself from the strength of those arms alone. "So is there real food too, or do I just eat apple pie for the entire meal?"

"Nope, you're gonna sit down and have a good-size burger and some fries, and then we'll give you a piece of pie to top it off."

He hadn't been terribly hungry when he walked in, but just the sound of that made his mouth water. Obligingly he went to the table she pointed out and sat down. Within seconds he had a hot cup of coffee in front of him. "What brings you into town?" she asked.

"What makes you think I'm new?" he asked, looking around. "I used to come through here often, promising I'd stop in to test the gossip about the best pies ever, but I never did. And I haven't been through this town in many years."

"This is a small community. I know every person who lives here. The rest are mostly passing through."

"Well, if they know about all those baked goods up under that glass," he said, "I wouldn't be at all surprised if everybody goes out of their way to come here."

She chuckled. "Enough that I make a fine living here," she said with a smirk, and she disappeared into the back kitchen. He could hear her talking to somebody and wondered if it was a mom-and-pop place. She came back out soon with cutlery and a glass of water. "You never answered my question."

"I'm tracking down a dog," he said.

"Purebred? For breeding?"

Surprised by that line of questioning, he shook his head. "No, she's a War Dog, shipped home with her handler. He ended up going to rehab and had multiple surgeries, then his wife left him. Since he can't live on his own, the dog got lost somewhere in all that."

"Pete Lowery," she said abruptly.

Startled, he look up at her. "Sorry?"

"Are you looking for Pete Lowery's dog, Salem?"

He frowned, pulled up his phone, checked the notes and said, "Yes, I am." He twisted to look up at her. "Do you know where the dog is?"

"It attacked somebody," she said, staring at him hard. He didn't know what she was looking for, but her gaze searched his, as if to see which way he would go on the issue.

His heart sank. "Seriously?"

She nodded, her face grave. "I'm not exactly sure what happened, but she bit a man in the leg," she said. "She might still be down at the police security yard, locked up," she said. "There was some talk about putting her down, but I haven't heard the outcome on that."

"Who could I talk to about it?"

"You'll have to talk to the sheriff," she said. "Give him about a half hour, and he'll probably pop in here for coffee and pie." And, with a smirk, she left again.

Pierce sat here, slowly stirring his black coffee to help it cool and wondered what would make a dog like that attack someone. Most likely a scenario where the dog was cornered and felt threatened or somebody she cared about was threatened. Pierce frowned, thinking about that until Aunt Marge came back out with a heaping plate of burger and fries. Curious, he asked, "Do you know the story behind the dog attack?"

"Something to do with Pete's brother, I think," she said. "Rob said the dog didn't do anything wrong, but two guys were just talking to him, and apparently the shepherd took a dislike to one of them and attacked him."

"Dogs often see a threat we don't quite understand," Pierce said in a neutral voice.

"I don't know all the details," she said with a shrug, walking over to the counter, returning with mustard and ketchup for him.

He nodded his thanks and picked up a fry and crunched it. He loved crispy fries. And these were hot and tasty. He dumped ketchup on his plate and proceeded to plow through the fries. When he was almost done, he picked up the burger and slowly worked his way through the beefy sandwich.

The meal was excellent. He'd come back just for the food. Aunt Marge returned, refilled his coffee and his water, but she didn't stop to talk this time. A couple other customers came and went, so it was steady but not terribly busy. Pierce was just about done with his burger, putting the last of it into his mouth, when a sheriff's car drove up. Pierce wondered at the timing. The sheriff was a bit early today apparently. Aunt Marge greeted him as he sat down and poured him a cup of coffee, then pointed over at Pierce and said, "He needs to talk to you about Salem."

The sheriff snorted. "If there was ever a dog that deserved a bullet, it's her," he said. He looked straight at Pierce and said, "If you come to collect her, you're too late. Somebody already stole her from the yard."

Aunt Marge gasped. "What? Now who'd do that?"

Peirce studied the sheriff's face. "Any idea who or when?"

"A couple months back," he said. "And, no, we have no clue who. Cut the fence and let her free. Hope they took her out back and put a bullet between her eyes. That's all she's good for."

Aunt Marge nodded in agreement. "So true. Last thing we need around here is dogs attacking innocent people."

Or rather people attacking dogs, Pierce thought to himself. But no use getting into that discussion here and now. Not until he knew the full story. But there were two things he did know: men attacked others without provocation, and dogs only attacked out of need.

Pierce highly doubted the dog would get an honest hearing with the sheriff though. That man had already made up his mind.

This concludes Book 1 of The K9 Files: Ethan.
Read about Pierce: The K9 Files, Book 2

THE K9 FILES: PIERCE (BOOK #2)

Just because helping out is the right thing to do doesn't make it easy ...

Pierce is on the hunt for Salem, a K9 military dog that belonged to Pete, a veteran, who can no longer look after himself or the dog. So the dog has been handed from owner to owner—until she's become too much to handle—and now the law is involved. No one has Salem's best interests in mind ... and they definitely don't have Pete's either. Pierce is about to change all that ... whether they like it or not.

Hedi, a young deputy, has lived in Arrowhead, Colorado, all her life and knows Pete and Salem but was helpless to do much when greed overtook his friends and family. She recognizes in Pierce the same qualities that Pete has, and, by Pierce's actions alone, she knows a corner has been turned. She also understands the locals won't take it lying down, and this means war ...

Pierce served his country overseas for many years, and seeing another veteran in trouble makes him realize the fight isn't over, even after life in the navy ends. In fact, this battle has just begun. But ... this one ... Pierce will finish. And he plans to win.

Book 2 is available now!

To find out more visit Dale Mayer's website.

http://smarturl.it/PierceDMUniversal

Author's Note

Thank you for reading Ethan: The K9 Files, Book 1! If you enjoyed the book, please take a moment and leave a short review.

Dear reader,

I love to hear from readers, and you can contact me at my website: www.dalemayer.com or at my Facebook author page. To be informed of new releases and special offers, sign up for my newsletter or follow me on BookBub. And if you are interested in joining Dale Mayer's Reader Group, here is the Facebook sign up page.
facebook.com/groups/402384989872660

Cheers,
Dale Mayer

Get THREE Free Books Now!

Have you met the SEALS of Honor?

SEALs of Honor Books 1, 2, and 3. Follow the stories of brave, badass warriors who serve their country with honor and love their women to the limits of life and death.

Read Mason, Hawk, and Dane right now for FREE.

Go here and tell me where to send them!
http://smarturl.it/EthanBofB

About the Author

Dale Mayer is a USA Today bestselling author best known for her Psychic Visions and Family Blood Ties series. Her contemporary romances are raw and full of passion and emotion (Second Chances, SKIN), her thrillers will keep you guessing (By Death series), and her romantic comedies will keep you giggling (It's a Dog's Life and Charmin Marvin Romantic Comedy series).

She honors the stories that come to her – and some of them are crazy and break all the rules and cross multiple genres!

To go with her fiction, she also writes nonfiction in many different fields with books available on resume writing, companion gardening and the US mortgage system. She has recently published her Career Essentials Series. All her books are available in print and ebook format.

Connect with Dale Mayer Online

Dale's Website – www.dalemayer.com
Twitter – @DaleMayer
Facebook – dalemayer.com/fb
BookBub – bookbub.com/authors/dale-mayer

Also by Dale Mayer

Published Adult Books:

The K9 Files
Ethan, Book 1
Pierce, Book 2

Lovely Lethal Gardens
Arsenic in the Azaleas, Book 1
Bones in the Begonias, Book 2
Corpse in the Carnations, Book 3
Daggers in the Dahlias, Book 4
Evidence in the Echinacea, Book 5
Footprints in the Ferns, Book 6

Psychic Vision Series
Tuesday's Child
Hide 'n Go Seek
Maddy's Floor
Garden of Sorrow
Knock Knock...
Rare Find
Eyes to the Soul
Now You See Her
Shattered
Into the Abyss
Seeds of Malice

Eye of the Falcon
Itsy-Bitsy Spider
Unmasked
Deep Beneath
Psychic Visions Books 1–3
Psychic Visions Books 4–6
Psychic Visions Books 7–9

By Death Series
Touched by Death
Haunted by Death
Chilled by Death
By Death Books 1–3

Broken Protocols – Romantic Comedy Series
Cat's Meow
Cat's Pajamas
Cat's Cradle
Cat's Claus
Broken Protocols 1-4

Broken and... Mending
Skin
Scars
Scales (of Justice)
Broken but... Mending 1-3

Glory
Genesis
Tori
Celeste
Glory Trilogy

Biker Blues

Morgan: Biker Blues, Volume 1

Cash: Biker Blues, Volume 2

SEALs of Honor

Mason: SEALs of Honor, Book 1

Hawk: SEALs of Honor, Book 2

Dane: SEALs of Honor, Book 3

Swede: SEALs of Honor, Book 4

Shadow: SEALs of Honor, Book 5

Cooper: SEALs of Honor, Book 6

Markus: SEALs of Honor, Book 7

Evan: SEALs of Honor, Book 8

Mason's Wish: SEALs of Honor, Book 9

Chase: SEALs of Honor, Book 10

Brett: SEALs of Honor, Book 11

Devlin: SEALs of Honor, Book 12

Easton: SEALs of Honor, Book 13

Ryder: SEALs of Honor, Book 14

Macklin: SEALs of Honor, Book 15

Corey: SEALs of Honor, Book 16

Warrick: SEALs of Honor, Book 17

Tanner: SEALs of Honor, Book 18

Jackson: SEALs of Honor, Book 19

Kanen: SEALs of Honor, Book 20

Nelson: SEALs of Honor, Book 21

SEALs of Honor, Books 1–3

SEALs of Honor, Books 4–6

SEALs of Honor, Books 7–10

SEALs of Honor, Books 11–13

SEALs of Honor, Books 14–16

SEALs of Honor, Books 17–19

Heroes for Hire

Levi's Legend: Heroes for Hire, Book 1

Stone's Surrender: Heroes for Hire, Book 2

Merk's Mistake: Heroes for Hire, Book 3

Rhodes's Reward: Heroes for Hire, Book 4

Flynn's Firecracker: Heroes for Hire, Book 5

Logan's Light: Heroes for Hire, Book 6

Harrison's Heart: Heroes for Hire, Book 7

Saul's Sweetheart: Heroes for Hire, Book 8

Dakota's Delight: Heroes for Hire, Book 9

Michael's Mercy (Part of Sleeper SEAL Series)

Tyson's Treasure: Heroes for Hire, Book 10

Jace's Jewel: Heroes for Hire, Book 11

Rory's Rose: Heroes for Hire, Book 12

Brandon's Bliss: Heroes for Hire, Book 13

Liam's Lily: Heroes for Hire, Book 14

North's Nikki: Heroes for Hire, Book 15

Anders's Angel: Heroes for Hire, Book 16

Reyes's Raina: Heroes for Hire, Book 17

Dezi's Diamond: Heroes for Hire, Book 18

Vince's Vixen: Heroes for Hire, Book 19

Heroes for Hire, Books 1–3

Heroes for Hire, Books 4–6

Heroes for Hire, Books 7–9

SEALs of Steel

Badger: SEALs of Steel, Book 1

Erick: SEALs of Steel, Book 2

Cade: SEALs of Steel, Book 3

Talon: SEALs of Steel, Book 4

Laszlo: SEALs of Steel, Book 5

Geir: SEALs of Steel, Book 6

Jager: SEALs of Steel, Book 7
The Final Reveal: SEALs of Steel, Book 8

Collections
Dare to Be You…
Dare to Love…
Dare to be Strong…
RomanceX3

Standalone Novellas
It's a Dog's Life
Riana's Revenge
Second Chances

Published Young Adult Books:

Family Blood Ties Series
Vampire in Denial
Vampire in Distress
Vampire in Design
Vampire in Deceit
Vampire in Defiance
Vampire in Conflict
Vampire in Chaos
Vampire in Crisis
Vampire in Control
Vampire in Charge
Family Blood Ties Set 1–3
Family Blood Ties Set 1–5
Family Blood Ties Set 4–6
Family Blood Ties Set 7–9
Sian's Solution, A Family Blood Ties Series Prequel

Novelette

Design series
Dangerous Designs
Deadly Designs
Darkest Designs
Design Series Trilogy

Standalone
In Cassie's Corner
Gem Stone (a Gemma Stone Mystery)
Time Thieves

Published Non-Fiction Books:

Career Essentials
Career Essentials: The Résumé
Career Essentials: The Cover Letter
Career Essentials: The Interview
Career Essentials: 3 in 1